Making Friends with the Enemy

"Oh, Lila, thank you so much for letting me ride your horse," Elizabeth said. "He's so special. I wish I had one just like him."

"Funny, that's what everybody says about him," Lila said. "I had three girls over to ride Thunder last week. None of them rode him as well as you. You know, I just can't let everyone ride my horse. Some of the grossest girls have asked me. I mean, a couple of them would scare Thunder away!"

Just play along with her, Elizabeth thought. "Like who?"

"Oh, you know, the usual nerds. Cammi Adams, Grace Oliver. Before you know it, people like Amy Sutton will be on my back."

Elizabeth stiffened. "You know, Lila, Amy is a friend of mine."

"Well, excu-u-u-se me! You have to admit, she is kind of strange."

At that point Elizabeth was so angry, she felt like slapping Lila. But a nagging thought stopped her: Don't blow it now, or you'll never see that horse again. . . .

D1375442

Bantam Books in the SWEET VALLEY TWINS series.
Ask your bookseller for the books you have missed.

SWEET VALLEY TWINS

First Place

Written by
Jamie Suzanne

Created by
FRANCINE PASCAL

A BANTAM BOOK®

TORONTO • NEW YORK • LONDON • SYDNEY • AUCKLAND

RL 4, 008–012

FIRST PLACE
A Bantam Book/December 1987
Reprinted 1988, 1990

Sweet Valley High is a registered trademark of Francine Pascal.

Sweet Valley Twins is a trademark of Francine Pascal.

Conceived by Francine Pascal.

Produced by Cloverdale Press Inc.

Cover art by James Mathewuse.

ISBN 0-553-15510-5

Printed and bound in Great Britain by
Cox & Wyman Ltd., Reading

First Place

One

"So, then, we see that the, uh, the ancient Greek city-states were the . . . the cradle, so to speak, of modern civilization."

As Mr. Nydick droned on, Jessica Wakefield sat eagerly writing in her loose-leaf notebook. Anyone dropping in on the sixth-grade history class would have thought that she was Mr. Nydick's best student. But her twin sister Elizabeth knew better. As soon as the teacher turned to face the blackboard, Jessica quickly folded her paper and slipped it onto her sister's desk.

Although Elizabeth hated being distracted from her schoolwork, she glanced at Jessica's note anyway. "He probably knows all about it because he was there!" it said. Elizabeth tried to glare disapprovingly at Jessica, but when their eyes met they both giggled.

"I'm sorry, did someone . . . eh . . . say something?" said Mr. Nydick, as he turned around, squinting. Elizabeth and Jessica immediately looked as innocent as babies. Shrugging his shoulders, Mr. Nydick turned back to the blackboard.

The two girls squirmed in their seats and tried to keep straight faces. The sunlight cast a warm glow on their long blond hair, and dark lashes framed their blue-green eyes. They were identical, right down to the dimples in their left cheeks.

Only their family and closest friends knew about their differences, like the small mole on Elizabeth's right shoulder and the fact that Elizabeth was born four minutes before her twin. The easiest way to tell them apart, though, was by their personalities. As Elizabeth tried valiantly to keep interested in what Mr. Nydick was saying, her sister couldn't have cared less. Jessica could never understand how someone identical to her could be so . . . so . . . well, *good*. Elizabeth loved reading, writing, long walks, and good conversation. To Jessica, life was all about having fun, and school was just an interruption.

But neither of the twins was having an easy time paying attention in this class. It was the last class of the day, and even Elizabeth found herself daydreaming. Her loose-leaf page was covered with drawings. Jessica peered over her sister's shoulder.

"What are those?" she whispered.

Elizabeth turned red. She didn't like talking during class. "Horses! Can't you tell?"

"What?"

"Horses!"

"Forces? Did somebody ask about forces?" Mr. Nydick peered around the room as he asked the question.

Jessica smiled mischievously as Elizabeth sank into her chair.

"Certainly, eh, the armies in ancient Greece played a large role in—"

Brrrring! The bell cut off Mr. Nydick and ended the school day. And not a moment too soon. The twins practically fell out the classroom door and exploded with laughter.

"Oh, I don't know how I held it in!" declared Jessica.

"You're terrible!" said Elizabeth between giggles. "How do you expect to learn anything?"

Jessica playfully raised an eyebrow. "And I suppose drawing horses is a good way to learn about the ancient Greeks?"

Elizabeth could only smile. When she looked into her sister's sparkling eyes, she couldn't imagine being closer to anyone in the world. Despite their differences, the Wakefield twins would always be the best of friends.

As they walked to their lockers, Jessica did a perfect imitation of Mr. Nydick, right down to the squint and stammer. It may have been cruel, but

Elizabeth doubled over and giggled. "Don't get me going, Jess," Elizabeth cried. She'd been laughing so hard her cheeks hurt. "You're going to make me late for my first riding lesson!"

Just as they turned the corner, they noticed a lot of commotion around the locker of Jessica's friend, Lila Fowler. Four or five of their sixth-grade classmates were gathered around Lila and chattering excitedly. "I wonder what's going on?" said Elizabeth. "I didn't even think Lila *knew* those girls."

"She didn't before this week," Jessica said with a knowing smile.

"So why is she so popular all of a sudden?"

"Didn't I tell you? She really got that horse she was talking about. Can you believe it? Now everyone wants to ride it!"

Lila's father was one of the richest men in Sweet Valley, and Elizabeth had gotten used to Lila's bragging about all the wonderful things she was going to ask him to buy her. But it seemed that half the time Lila would forget about asking him, and the other half she'd lose interest in the things even before she got them. So Elizabeth didn't pay much attention when Lila went around telling everyone she was getting a horse.

But it made Elizabeth suddenly feel strange to hear that Lila actually had one. Elizabeth had become passionate about horses lately, and it went beyond doodling in her notebook. She couldn't read enough about them, and she looked forward to starting riding lessons more than anything else.

"Anyway," Jessica continued with a sly grin, "I'm supposed to meet her to go to a Unicorn Club meeting. I just hope she can tear herself away from all her new friends." The Unicorns were a group of girls who thought they were beautiful and very special, just like Unicorns. Elizabeth had been to one of their meetings, and she thought the girls were boy-crazy gossips.

When Elizabeth spoke, her voice was subdued. "Well, I'll see you later, then. Have fun at your meeting." With that, she turned and walked quickly through the school doors.

"Jessica! Hi!" Lila waved from her locker. She threw back her shoulder-length light brown hair and flashed a wide, self-satisfied smile. As if trying to score points, the other girls all smiled and greeted her, too. "So what's new?" she asked as she walked over toward Jessica.

"Oh, nothing much. My sister's all excited about her new riding class today."

Lila rolled her eyes. "Oh, riding class. Yes, I've been to a few of those. What a pain!"

Lila then turned to her groupies and said, "Well, gotta go now. It's great to see you all. Oh, and, Melissa . . ." Her brown eyes looked with special meaning at one of the girls. "Thanks for the math homework last night. Why don't you come over this weekend and ride Thunder?"

As the group disbanded, the only one smiling was Melissa McCormick.

"Lila, this is amazing," said Jessica when the hallway had emptied. "I've never even seen half of those girls!"

"I hadn't either, until I got Thunder," Lila answered.

"You just love all the attention, don't you?" said Jessica.

"Who, *me*?" said Lila, looking around in mock disbelief. Both girls laughed.

"I'll bet all those girls just want to be invited to see Thunder! They're trying as hard as they can to be your best friend."

"And it looks like I may never have to do homework again. All I have to do is promise to let people ride him."

"At that rate, you'll never even have time to ride him yourself!"

"Believe me, Jessica, I can live without riding Thunder."

"But he's your own horse!" Jessica exclaimed in surprise. "Aren't you excited?"

"I guess. It's kind of fun to ride him, but the rest—*Yuck!* You constantly have to brush horses, and groom them, and clean up after them. And those creepy stableboys have no class at all . . ." Lila said in her most snobbish voice.

"Well, it was nice of your dad to buy you one. They're really expensive. My father looked at some a while back, when Elizabeth started getting interested in them."

Lila nodded her head but clearly wanted to change the subject. "Oh, I can't wait to show you the new necklace I told Daddy to buy me. It looks like it was just *made* for my new yellow silk blouse!"

As Lila described the necklace, Jessica was amazed at how quickly Lila had gotten over being excited about her horse.

Elizabeth headed straight home after riding class. She and Amy Sutton had planned to meet there to do homework together. Sure enough, when she arrived, Amy and Elizabeth's mother were walking around the outside of the Wakefields' pretty split-level ranch house. They were smelling the lemon blossoms, which had just started to open.

Elizabeth smiled when she saw them. This was one of the best things about living in Sweet Valley, California. Throughout the year, the air was filled with the wonderful scent of flowers. She couldn't imagine a more perfect place in the world. Just about every day had bright sun and blue skies, and the beach was only a bike ride away.

"Look who's here! Are you bowlegged yet?" Peering through the front screen door was Elizabeth's fourteen-year-old brother, Steven. As always, he was a master of the unneeded comment.

"No, and I'm not skinheaded, either," she answered good-naturedly. Steven had just gotten a very short haircut, and Elizabeth's retort hit him right where it hurt.

Mrs. Wakefield and Amy chuckled. Elizabeth gave her mother a big hug and took a long, luxurious whiff of the flowers.

"How was class?" asked Mrs. Wakefield.

"Oh, Mom, it was unbelievable. My teacher, Mrs. Fairmont, is so sweet and patient. And I fell in love with some of those horses."

"I'm glad! Did they give you a good one to ride?"

"Yes, she's a beautiful piebald, just like the one in *National Velvet*!"

Elizabeth sensed that Amy was not interested in the conversation. She turned to her and said, "You think we can finish this book report tonight?"

"If we decide not to sleep!" Amy replied with a deadpan look. Amy was Elizabeth's best friend, and Elizabeth loved her sense of humor. With her stringy blond hair and athletic build, Amy was something of a tomboy. She wasn't glamorous or popular like Jessica's Unicorn friends, but they had accepted her into their Booster squad because she was such a good baton-twirler. Elizabeth thought Amy was one of the nicest people she had ever met.

"Well, it sounds like you two had better get rolling before it's dinnertime," said Mrs. Wakefield. The girls went inside the house.

Elizabeth's bedroom was a perfect place to study. She kept it clean and neat, and there were plenty of big pillows to sit on. The cream-colored walls with blue trim made the room feel peaceful and comfortable. On one wall was a small framed picture of the greatest race horse of all, Man-of-War. Over her bed was a poster of the wild ponies of Chincoteague running on the beach. By her bed was an open copy of *National Velvet*. The two friends settled in for their study session.

Elizabeth and Amy had already gotten a lot done when there was a knock on the door. "It's awfully quiet in there. Are you doing your homework or taking a nap?" The door opened and Jessica peeked in.

"Come on in, Jess," said her twin. "We've almost finished our book reports."

"Yeah, let's take a break," Amy piped up.

"Book report?" Jessica said, wide-eyed. "What book are you writing about, Elizabeth?"

"*National Velvet*," she answered.

"Really? That's the book I was going to do *my* report on! Let's see what you have."

Uh-oh, thought Elizabeth, *here we go again.* She could always tell when her sister was trying to get around doing her own homework. "I'll tell you what," she said, "we'll talk about it later, and you can give us some ideas of your own. We want to take a break for a few minutes."

That was fine with Jessica. Taking breaks was her style. "Well, guess what? I'm going to see Lila's horse on Saturday!"

"Along with about seven million other girls, probably," said Amy. "Lila's become Miss Popularity since she got that horse," she continued.

Jessica shook her head in wonder. "Can you imagine, she doesn't even really care about it! She mentioned it one day to her father on a whim, and the next week they were visiting stables. By the time he picked one out and brought it home, I think she'd even forgotten that she'd asked him for it!"

"That's Lila," said Amy, shrugging her shoulders.

Elizabeth became gloomy all of a sudden. "What could she possibly want with a horse?" she said. "All she's interested in is boys and clothes. She probably won't even take care of the poor thing."

"Lizzie, you sound jealous!" said Jessica.

Elizabeth forced a smile. "Don't be silly. I'm just tired. Riding class was really hard today."

But underneath it all, Elizabeth couldn't get one thought out of her head: *Why, of all people, does Lila get a horse when I'm the one who really deserves one?*

Two
◇

Elizabeth was the only girl writing during lunch period the next day. It was the day of the school newspaper deadline. Elizabeth was in charge of the *Sweet Valley Sixers*, the sixth-grade paper, and that meant long hours of work in her spare time. On deadline days it meant giving up lunch.

At that moment she was stuck. She couldn't think of a good headline for a story about a teacher who liked to take balloon trips on weekends. Suddenly she heard Lila in the lunch line.

"No, Mrs. Whitney, take the cream sauce *off* my chicken cutlet. You want me to develop cellulite at my age?"

The headline hit Elizabeth and she scribbled it down: "Going Places with Hot Air." *Thank you, Lila*, she thought with a smile.

Within moments Elizabeth was forced to

gather up her papers. Lila sat down at the other end of the table, and a group of girls took seats around her. Most of them were trying to get Lila's attention and didn't even notice Elizabeth. Their questions overlapped one another.

"Why did you name him Thunder?"

"Where is his stable?"

"What color is he?"

"Chestnut? Is that like brown?"

"How old is he?"

It was impossible to concentrate. The last thing Elizabeth wanted was to sit next to a bunch of girls jabbering about Lila's horse. And even worse, Lila was just sitting smugly like a princess before ladies-in-waiting. Elizabeth picked up her pile to move to another table.

"Oh, Elizabeth! Are we in your way?" asked Lila in a voice that said she really didn't care.

"Well, the *Sweet Valley Sixers* deadline is today, and I'm way behind. But it's no problem. I'll just move over to the corner table."

Lila nodded and turned to her friends. Then, all at once, her face lit up as if she had been struck with a wonderful idea. She sprang out of her seat. "Here, let me help you," she said, sounding concerned. "These girls have *no* respect for your privacy!"

She went around the table and carefully lifted a stack of papers for Elizabeth, while the other girls looked on. Elizabeth couldn't understand this sudden change of attitude, but something smelled fishy.

"Uh, thanks, Lila, you really didn't have to do that," Elizabeth said.

"It's no problem, Liz. I don't want to keep you from finishing up the newspaper. It's one of my *favorite* things about school. What articles are going to be in this issue?"

"Well, there's a story about the Booster Club and a feature about Mr. Glennon's balloon trip . . ." With a pang of guilt, she quietly placed her arm over the headline she had just written.

"Wow! How *interesting*! I can't wait to read them!" Lila exclaimed.

What is going on here? Elizabeth thought. "OK, Lila, thanks for helping, but I—"

Lila cut her off. "Listen, I know you're real busy, but when do you start thinking of articles for the next issue?"

"We're already thinking of them. Why?"

"Do you ever take suggestions from anyone?"

"Sure. It's a newspaper for all the sixth graders."

"Great!" Lila leaned over the table and gave Elizabeth her most magnetic smile. "I have a fantastic idea. Why don't you do an article on my new horse, Thunder? You've never had an article about a horse. And think how many girls would want to read about him!"

You mean, think how many girls would see your

name in print, Elizabeth thought. "That *is* an idea, Lila. But I think space is already looking tight for that issue."

"Oh. Well, think about it, OK?"

Elizabeth nodded politely and turned back to her work.

"By the way," Lila added, "why don't you come over to the stable tomorrow and meet Thunder? I just asked Jessica, and she said she'd come."

It was getting harder and harder for Elizabeth to cover up her annoyance. "Thanks, Lila, but I've got a lot of homework to do."

"On a Saturday?" Lila said with a sneer, which she quickly covered up. "I understand. You sure are busy! Maybe some other time."

As Lila walked back to her seat, Elizabeth was fuming. When the bell rang at the end of lunch period, she gathered up her work and stormed into the hallway, head down.

"Hey, watch where you're going!" Elizabeth looked up to see that she had almost run into her sister and Betsy Gordon.

"Sorry, Jess!" Even though she didn't mean it, her voice sounded as though she were snapping at Jessica.

"Wait a minute! What's wrong?"

Elizabeth cast a tortured glance at her sister. "We'll talk about it later." With that, she walked off.

* * *

Jessica went right to Elizabeth's room when she got home from her Unicorn Club meeting after school.

"Lizzie?" Jessica said tentatively. She opened the door to find Elizabeth sitting on her bed, a sad expression on her face. "Look at you!" Jessica declared. "You look like the world is coming to an end. What's the matter?" She sat down next to Elizabeth and put her arm around her.

"Jessica, I will never, *never* write an article about Lila and her crummy horse! How *dare* she ask me?"

"Is *that* what's bothering you? Oh, Lizzie, don't take Lila so seriously. She's just trying to show off. That's the way she is!"

"I know, but she's just such a phony. I mean, today at lunch she pretended to be all friendly with me. She just wanted to butter me up so I would write a story about her." Elizabeth's face turned red with anger.

"Look, why don't we ask Mom and Dad to take us to Casey's Place for ice cream? Then let's just go to sleep and by tomorrow you'll forget the whole thing. OK?"

Elizabeth smiled at her sister. Usually Jessica was the one who needed a shoulder to cry on. It made Elizabeth feel warm inside to know that she could depend on Jessica, too. "OK."

After a good night's sleep, Elizabeth's anger seemed to melt away. She woke up late Saturday morning, feeling refreshed. Jessica was at the stable with Lila, and Mr. and Mrs. Wakefield were busy around the house. Now would be a good time to be alone and sort out her feelings.

Elizabeth strolled out to one of her favorite spots in the backyard—her "thinking seat" a low branch of the old pine tree. She used to share this spot with Jessica, until Jessica felt she was too old for it. To Elizabeth, there was no better place for serious thought.

There sure was a lot to think about. Elizabeth wondered why she was taking this thing with Lila so seriously. How could she have been so rude to her in school? Was Jessica right about her? Maybe Lila wasn't so bad. All these things went through Elizabeth's mind as she breathed in the strong, sweet smell of pine and gazed into the sky.

She wasn't aware how much time had passed when the pounding of running footsteps broke her concentration.

"There you are, Lizzie! Didn't you hear me calling you?"

"Sorry, Jess, I must have been daydreaming. It's so beautiful today, isn't it?"

The last thing Jessica wanted to talk about was the weather. "Well, you really missed something incredible this morning. Lila may brag a lot, but this time—Oh, boy! Liz, that horse is *gorgeous*! You would absolutely adore it!"

Elizabeth raised her eyebrows, and the corners of her mouth turned up. She was feeling more calm about the subject of Lila's horse. "Really? I thought you didn't like horses."

"I don't! But even I can't resist this one. He's . . . he's . . . I just can't describe him! Oh, I wish you didn't dislike Lila so much. You should see him! Look at it this way—you two finally have *something* in common!"

"Maybe you're right," Elizabeth said. Then she sighed. "But at this point, Lila probably thinks I'm the biggest snob in the world."

"No way!" Jessica insisted. "Besides, I told her you'd go crazy over Thunder if you saw him. And she seemed really excited about that."

"Yeah? So you think I should be friendlier?"

"Why not? Talk to her. Tell her . . . I know! Tell her you'll write that newspaper article."

Elizabeth hadn't thought about going that far. But, on second thought, maybe it wasn't such a bad idea.

Three

◇

When Elizabeth walked into Sweet Valley Middle School that Monday morning, her mind was made up. She held her head high as she passed Lila at her locker.

"Morning, Lila."

"Another Monday, what a pain in the—" Lila stopped short when she saw who it was. "Oh, hi! I didn't know that was you, Elizabeth. We missed you on Saturday."

"Jessica told me all about Thunder. Sounds like he's beautiful. What is he, a quarter horse?"

"Yeah, I think that's what they call him at the stable. I'd still love for you to come see him."

She doesn't even know what kind of a horse she has! Elizabeth told herself in disbelief. "Well, to tell you the truth, I have an even better idea."

"What?"

"I've been thinking about that article you suggested. You're right, you know. We *haven't* had a horse article. It's a terrific idea. In fact, I'd like to write it myself."

Lila looked as though she had just won a trip to Tahiti. Her eyes became large and her face flushed. "I just *knew* you'd think so! Will I be able to get copies to send to all my friends from camp, and my aunt and uncle in San Diego, and—"

"Hold on there a minute!" Elizabeth said with a chuckle. "Let's write the thing first. If we don't plan some meeting times now, there may not even be an article."

"Oh. Yes, of course. Well, how about today after school? The stable isn't too far away."

"Sounds good. I'll meet you in the lobby by the pay phones at three o'clock."

Done, Elizabeth thought. *She'll get the publicity she wants, and I'll get to see Thunder. And after the article, I'll never have to deal with her again.*

Throughout the rest of the day, though, Elizabeth became more excited. The clock hands couldn't move fast enough, especially in Mr. Nydick's class. She clenched and unclenched her pencil as the old teacher went on and on about the ancient Greeks.

"Psst!" Elizabeth heard a familiar sound. Sure enough, Jessica was slipping a folded note onto her desk. Elizabeth quietly opened it up to read: "What room did the black stallion check into when he went to a hotel?"

Before Elizabeth could even think about Jessica's riddle, the long-awaited bell sounded. She was off like a racehorse from a starting gate.

She was the first person in the school lobby. Before long, the lobby was crowded with rushing, boisterous students. It became hard to avoid being bumped.

"Excuse me!" came a voice from behind her.

Elizabeth spun around with a big smile. "Li—"

A small, dark brown-haired girl asked, "Do you have change for a dollar?"

Well, the voice *sounded* like Lila's.

"I think so," Elizabeth said, and she quickly searched around in her purse.

"Aren't you Elizabeth Wakefield, the one in charge of the *Sweet Valley Sixers*?" the girl asked.

"Mm-hm." Elizabeth nodded. She handed the girl four quarters.

The girl's eyes sparkled. "My name is Sophia Rizzo. I think you do a great job, and I'm wondering if I could maybe join—"

"Sure, sure," Elizabeth interrupted. "Just come to our next meeting. We'll post the date on the front door next week." She could tell at once that she liked this girl, but *now* was not the time to chat.

"Great! See you then!" Sophia said as she turned to the phone.

Elizabeth kept looking out for Lila. But after fifteen minutes, the crowd had disappeared. Elizabeth shuffled toward the front door. *I should have known Lila would forget*, she thought.

Elizabeth took one look back at the empty lobby and pushed open the glass door.

"Hey, wait! Where are you going? Don't you want to do the article?" There was no mistaking *this* voice.

"Lila! I thought you'd left."

"Left? You said to meet by the phones at three o'clock. It's only twenty after three now."

"Lila—" Realizing it was no use, Elizabeth cut herself short. Obviously, that line of reasoning made perfect sense to Lila. And if Elizabeth wanted to see Thunder, she'd just have to put up with her for a while. "Shall we go?"

"Mm-hm. I swear, I don't know *why* I just spent all that time doing my hair when all I'm going to see are those awful stableboys."

The walk to the stable was longer than Elizabeth had expected. Although Lila complained once or twice that they should have called a cab, Elizabeth didn't mind at all. She just kept thinking of what was at the end of their walk.

Elizabeth had always been fascinated by the size of the houses in this neighborhood. The lawns seemed to stretch endlessly. As they turned a corner, a soft gust of wind caressed their faces. With it came a pungent aroma familiar to both girls.

"Ooh, we're near the stable, aren't we, Lila?" Elizabeth said.

"*Yuck*. I can *never* get this stink out of my clothes."

And there, on a white fence behind a lush group of palm trees, was a wooden sign that said Carson Stable. Elizabeth ran to the fence and gazed around.

"Oh, Lila, this is huge! It's nothing like the place where I take lessons!"

Lila gave a halfhearted grin as Elizabeth took it all in. There were several huge buildings, each one with beautiful redwood planking. The biggest ones had sloping roofs with raised midsections.

Elizabeth had read about this stable, but she had never imagined it would be so lovely. The pasture seemed to disappear into the distant mist, and the stable buildings looked like a quaint little town. There were two smaller paddocks near the stall buildings, along with an outdoor grooming area. On the left she saw a couple of rings, one with bleachers and some jumps set up inside.

"Well, don't just stand there, Elizabeth. Let's go in."

Lila led Elizabeth into one of the large

wooden buildings. Once inside, Elizabeth was intoxicated by the smell of hay and leather and horse.

A high-school-age boy with pimples was mucking out a stall. He smiled pleasantly when he saw Lila. "Hey! Another friend from school?"

"Calm down, George. This is my friend Elizabeth."

"Nice to meet you, Liz," said George. "You'll like Thunder." He turned to Lila. "I just finished his stall for you. I'll go get him."

As George steered the wheelbarrow out of the building, Lila indicated what she thought of him. She crossed her eyes, held her nose, and placed two fingers into her open mouth. Elizabeth smiled politely and thought, *Very funny. OK, let's get this over with. It'll be fun to see the horse. We'll do the article, and—*

At that moment, an older stablehand brought in a horse that made Elizabeth's jaw drop. She had never seen anything like it in her life. His sorrel coat glowed like the embers of a waning fire, and his broad chest heaved evenly with his footsteps. With one glance of his steady brown eyes, he seemed to peer into Elizabeth's soul.

"'Scuse me," the stablehand called out, "you know whose chestnut this is?"

"Mine," said Lila. "Elizabeth, meet Thunder."

Four

◇

Nothing that Jessica said had prepared Elizabeth for her meeting with Thunder. In the silence of her first glance, she felt she could barely breathe. His eyes looked almost human, with a deep, calm intelligence. And when he stared at her, he seemed to be saying, "Yes. You're the one."

He gave a regal nod, and Elizabeth admired the perfect slope of his neck, rising like a tree trunk from his forequarters. His long shoulder muscles glistened as they stretched tightly up to the withers. And his legs, which tapered beautifully to their hooves, seemed graceful yet powerful.

"He's . . . he's . . . stunning," said Elizabeth, at a loss for a word that could truly describe what she saw.

"Yeah, my dad says he's the best one in the stable. Would you like to ride him?"

"*Would* I!" Elizabeth said with gleaming eyes and a huge smile.

"OK. Well, I have a spare set of riding clothes in a room in the main office building. They'll let you change there."

Within seconds Elizabeth was in the changing room, clothes in hand. Lila's "spare set of riding clothes" was nothing less than a Stetson, a wool-challis shirt with a matching silk bandana, riding pants, a belt with a mother-of-pearl buckle, a buckskin vest, shotgun chaps, and custom-made calfskin polo boots, all of it hardly ever worn.

Although the boots were a little snug, Lila's clothes weren't a bad fit. Elizabeth walked back to the stable.

"You look sensational," said Lila.

"But I only know how to ride English," said Elizabeth.

"That's OK. It's just a spare outfit. Besides, they're much better-looking!"

George had come back in and saddled Thunder in the meantime. He smiled warmly at Elizabeth. "There's a class just starting in the ring, so let's take him out to the pasture."

The three of them walked outside, with George leading the horse by his reins. When they got to the pasture, Elizabeth went up to Thunder and stroked his mane timidly.

"Hi there, big guy. I'm Elizabeth," she said in a soft voice.

"No need to be afraid. He's very good with strangers," said George. "The last girl who owned him went off to college, and she used to have all her friends ride him."

Elizabeth looked at Thunder's alert and peaceful face, and whatever fear she had vanished. She mounted him and sat deep in the saddle. While George adjusted the stirrups, she took the reins and thought of all the things she had learned in riding class: Shoulders back and open. Weight on the heels, toes up. Fingers closed on the reins, thumbs to the sky. Separate the hands, bend the elbows, carry the forearms. Keep the knees in and tuck the seat under. Have positive rein contact and drive with the lower leg . . . There was so much to remember!

"OK, he's all yours," said George.

Elizabeth squeezed with her legs and made clicking noises. Thunder responded to her cues immediately, with a feeling of lightness that Elizabeth hadn't experienced on her riding-class horse. In an instant, she stopped thinking so hard about what to do. It all seemed to come naturally. She felt as though she were meant to ride Thunder.

She brought the horse to a trot. Even though she was posting clumsily in the saddle, the horse didn't seem to mind. He gave her an even, rolling ride along the edge of the pasture.

"Bring him to a canter! He has a great one!" shouted George.

Elizabeth hadn't learned how to go to a canter yet, but she'd watched another class do it. She knew that it was easier to go to a canter from a walk, so she carefully slowed Thunder down, and began to have second thoughts. What if she messed this up? Would she know how to control him?

Her doubts lasted only a few seconds. She gave Thunder a good, hard kick and he took off. The ride was smooth and easy.

Suddenly Elizabeth panicked as they approached the far corner. *What did the instructor say about taking a bend?* she thought frantically. *There was something about—Oh, yes! The instructor kept shouting, "Outside leg, inside rein!"*

They were almost at the corner. Elizabeth kicked with her right leg and pulled on the left rein. Without a hitch, Thunder took the left bend gracefully. Coming down the other side of the pasture, Elizabeth rode with new confidence. She cried out with joy as the scenery flew by her.

"Don't lean forward so much!" George yelled as Elizabeth came back around with Thunder.

She took his advice, and the next couple of rides around were even smoother and more wonderful than the first. When Elizabeth finally returned and dismounted, she was so excited that her feet barely touched the ground.

"You're a real pro! How long have you been taking lessons?" said George.

"Only one week."

"Not bad. He must really like you."

"George, would you be the world's sweetest guy and walk Thunder so he'll cool down?" asked Lila. "We have to get started on our newspaper article. Right, Liz?"

"Uh, yes. Good idea, Lila! I'll change and get my notebook. Nice to meet you, George. I'll see you around!"

"Not after this week. My family's moving, and someone else is taking my place. You and Lila take good care of Thunder, OK?"

Behind George's back, Lila signaled Elizabeth to hurry up, and Elizabeth rushed off.

The two girls walked back to Lila's house. "So we'll talk about me and my horse until dinnertime," said Lila. "Can you stay for dinner?"

"I'll call my mother and ask. Oh, Lila, thank you so much for letting me ride your horse. He's so special. I wish I had one just like him."

"Funny, that's what *everybody* says about him. I had three girls over to ride him last week. None of them rode him as well as you. Melissa McCormick was like a limp dishrag on top of him. Oh! Did you see the dress she was wearing today? Talk about ugly!"

Elizabeth really didn't feel like gossiping, but

she figured she'd tolerate it. After all, she *did* want to be invited to ride Thunder again.

"You know," Lila continued, "I just can't let everyone ride my horse. Some of the grossest girls have asked me. A couple of them would scare Thunder away!"

"Like who?" Elizabeth asked, deciding to play along with Lila.

"Oh, you know, the usual nerds. Cammi Adams, Grace Oliver—that type. Before you know it, people like Lois Waller and Amy Sutton will be on my back."

Elizabeth stiffened at the mention of Amy's name. "You know, Lila, Amy *is* a friend of mine."

"Well, excu-u-u-se *me*! I was just teasing. You have to admit, she *is* kind of strange."

At that point Elizabeth was so angry she felt like telling Lila to forget about the story. But a nagging thought stopped her from reacting: *Don't blow it now, or you'll never see that horse again.*

She decided the best thing to do was change the subject. "So, when did you get Thunder?"

They chatted the rest of the way home. Elizabeth vowed that, for the time being, she'd try to stay on Lila's good side.

By the following Tuesday, people noticed that Elizabeth and Lila were spending a lot more time together. Especially the Unicorns.

Betsy Gordon, Kimberly Haver, and Janet Howell were gossiping in the hallway between classes when Jessica approached. "It sure looks like your sister and Lila have become buddy-buddy," Kimberly said to Jessica. "I never would have thought . . ."

Jessica laughed. "You've got it all wrong. The only reason she spends so much time with Lila is because she's doing a newspaper article on her horse!"

All three girls murmured, "Oh," followed by an awkward silence. Then Betsy spoke up.

"I guess that's why she walks to school with her every morning, spends her lunch period writing with her, and goes to the stable with her after school every afternoon."

Jessica was beginning to feel annoyed at having to defend her twin. "Look, I'm telling you, we all know Lila is *not* my sister's type, OK? Elizabeth's just very dedicated to the *Sweet Valley Sixers* and really interested in horses. That's all! What's the big deal?"

Jessica said a quick goodbye and rushed down the hallway. She was late for her usual brief meeting time with Elizabeth before fifth period.

"Hi, Liz. Sorry I'm late. Gosh, could you understand *anything* Ms. Wyler said in math class today?"

"Sure," Elizabeth said with a smile. "It was easy!"

"Really? Well, maybe you could show me your homework tonight after you're finished?"

Elizabeth rolled her eyes and chuckled. She'd expected this. "Well, Jess, to tell you the truth, I told Lila I'd do the homework with her at her house after school. Want to come?"

"Uh, OK, sure. I'll meet you out front."

"Great. See you then. This'll be fun!"

As Elizabeth rushed off to class, Jessica felt strange. She'd never dreamed her sister would share her homework with Lila. As she walked slowly down the hallway, she began to think again about what her friends had said.

Five

Mr. Fowler's driver picked the girls up from school that day. During the ride, Lila couldn't stop mentioning a "surprise" she had in store for the twins.

"Lila," groaned Jessica, "if you're not going to tell us what it is, why even talk about it?"

"You're right, you're right . . ." Lila answered. "But boy, you'll be glad I did it!"

"Did *what*?" cried Elizabeth.

"Oh, nothing, nothing . . ."

The car pulled into the curved driveway and stopped in front of the Fowlers' Georgian house. Elizabeth admired the formal boxwood garden and the long, manicured lawn. But there was something missing, she thought. For all its perfect beauty, it just didn't look like the kind of place she could call home.

"Come on inside. I'm hungry!" Lila said. She

led the girls into the house and straight to the kitchen. On the counter was a large batch of moist, warm cookies that gave off an irresistible smell.

"Oh, no. Not oatmeal raisin again! Sometimes I think that's all Mrs. Pervis knows how to make."

Jessica gave Elizabeth an impish look and said, "That's all right, Lila. Liz and I love oatmeal raisin."

"Well, maybe I'll have just *one*." Lila took a cookie and went into the living room with the whole plate. Jessica and Elizabeth followed her.

Three-quarters of a plate of cookies later, Lila sprang up and announced, "OK, now it's time for the surprise."

She led the eager twins through several elegantly furnished rooms and out the rear door. There they saw a back lawn that was manicured as perfectly as the front, only twice as large. The palms and junipers seemed to twinkle in the crisp afternoon sun, and the pool was calm and inviting. But nothing about it seemed unusual.

Nothing, that is, except for the loud snort that erupted from a corner of the yard hidden by the pool's cabana.

"You didn't, Lila!" said Jessica in a loud whisper.

"Thunder!" cried Elizabeth as she ran behind the cabana.

Sure enough, there he was, tied to a tree and nodding his head. Elizabeth beamed.

"Lila, you weren't kidding. This is a surprise! What's he doing here?"

"Well, Elizabeth, I knew you were coming to help me with my homework, so I figured I would do something for you."

"How did you get him here?" Jessica asked.

"I called the stable and arranged to have him dropped off. They're going to pick him up later."

"That must be incredibly expensive," declared Jessica.

"Oh, Daddy won't mind. I just put it on his bill, and he never says anything."

Elizabeth looked around. Nearby was a bag of carrots and a currycomb that someone had brought out earlier. She fed a carrot to Thunder and watched his jaws snap it up. Then she picked up the currycomb and stroked Thunder's coat with a gentle, circular motion.

"Let's get some of the dirt out of this coat," she said warmly.

"Wouldn't it be great if they could breed a type of horse that doesn't need grooming?" Lila said.

Elizabeth laughed. "No. Grooming is fun! If I had a horse, I'd groom him every day. Besides, don't you think it's a good way for you to spend some time with Thunder? He really does like the attention."

"If you say so," Lila said. "But between you and me, it's the worst thing about having a horse."

"Well, if you did it more often, he wouldn't always need it so badly," Elizabeth answered.

Lila sighed. "If I could only find someone to do it for me! Someone who would also take care of his daily workouts—"

"I'll do it!" Elizabeth exclaimed without a moment's hesitation. She was thrilled to be able to do something in return for Lila's generosity with Thunder.

Jessica was surprised by her twin's eagerness, but Lila looked as though she had expected it all along.

"Great!" Lila said. "You can start tomorrow if you want." She looked at her watch. "Oops, it's getting late. Let's get started on this homework."

The three girls went inside to Lila's room and got to work. That is, Elizabeth did most of the work, and Lila and Jessica pretended to understand everything she told them. After a while, Lila began to look a bit uneasy and kept glancing at the time.

Just as Elizabeth was working on the last problem, the doorbell rang.

"Keep going, Elizabeth. We're almost done," Lila said as she rushed out of sight and opened the front door. A brief silence followed, and Elizabeth noticed some urgent whispering.

Lila reappeared at the bedroom door with one of the Unicorns, Ellen Riteman.

"Hi, Jessica and Elizabeth! How's it going?" Ellen asked.

Elizabeth was puzzled by Ellen's tense smile. "Oh, hi, Ellen. We're working on Ms. Wyler's homework. Have you done it yet?"

"Oh! Uh, no, I haven't. I was just dropping by to say hello to Lila. Is it hard?"

"Just the last two questions."

Ellen nodded uncomfortably, and all at once something dawned on Elizabeth.

She's here for the homework, she realized. *Lila probably told her I'd be gone by now, and she could copy the answers.*

Elizabeth's suspicions must have registered on her face, because Lila quickly pulled Ellen away and said, "Come on into the living room. I think we still have some cookies left."

Jessica was still puzzling over one of the math questions. "I can't figure out how you did number seven," she said.

Elizabeth tossed her notebook on the bed. "Here, look at my notes. I'm going to get a little fresh air."

She wandered into the backyard, lost in her thoughts. Amber light from the setting sun cast long shadows all around. The pool looked cold and empty, just the way Elizabeth felt.

At least she could have been honest and asked if Ellen could join us, Elizabeth thought. She'd never been that comfortable about sharing her homework with Lila, let alone with someone she hadn't given permission to.

Elizabeth was torn. On the one hand, she wanted to go inside and take her homework back from Lila. But each time she was about to do it, she was stopped by the thought of never getting to see Thunder again. That was the most unbearable thing she could imagine. She sighed. *Oh well, what's a little math homework anyway?* she thought.

Maybe seeing Thunder would cheer her up. The cabana was at the other end of the backyard, and she peered into the area behind it, which had now grown dark. As she got closer she could see the silhouette of the horse moving. Something about it didn't seem quite right. Elizabeth tiptoed up to the cabana.

Suddenly her eyes popped open. There was a boy back there. And he was quietly untying Thunder from the tree.

"Stop, thief!" Elizabeth cried.

Six

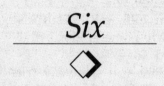

The back door swung open. Jessica, Lila, and Ellen darted out in a panic.

Behind the cabana, the boy spun around to face Elizabeth. He looked about fourteen years old, and scared.

"What?" he said. "Oh, uh, hi. Do you live here?"

"Get your hands off that horse before I call the police!" Elizabeth cried.

As the other girls reached Elizabeth's side, the confused boy sputtered, "No! You don't understand! I'm from Carson Stable!"

"How do we know you're telling the truth? *I* don't recognize you," said Lila. Just then the front doorbell chimed.

"I just started working there yesterday. That's my boss at your front door. He's got the horse van out front, and he sent me back here to get your horse. I'm sorry, I didn't mean to scare you!"

One look at his gentle and frightened face was enough for Elizabeth to know he was honest. This must be the boy who had replaced George. She smiled. "You took me by surprise. *I'm* sorry I scared *you*. My name is Elizabeth."

"I'm Ted Rog—"

"How dare you scare my friend like that?" Lila declared. "You couldn't wait with your boss at the front door? I'm going to complain to the stable about you!"

Ted was mortified. "Gee, I really didn't mean it. I'll never do it again."

"It's OK, Lila. He was just doing what he was told," Elizabeth said.

"What, can't he speak for himself?" Lila snapped and stormed into the house.

Ted turned to the others. He didn't look comfortable in the presence of so many girls. "Well, I guess there goes my new job."

"Don't worry," said Elizabeth. "She's not as bad as she seems."

"I hope not. I need this job to save up for college."

"Do you go to Sweet Valley High?" Jessica asked.

"Yes, I'm a freshman."

"Do you know our brother, Steven Wakefield?"

"No, but I've heard his name. He's on the basketball team, right?"

Jessica nodded.

Their conversation was cut short when Lila appeared with Ted's boss. He chuckled and clasped Ted playfully around the neck.

"So, I hear you made the girls think you were the masked horse bandit!"

Ted hung his head. "I'm sorry, Mr. Mansfield. I apologized to them."

"That's all right, son. Just a misunderstanding. Listen, it's getting late. I'll wait for you in the van while you bring him around."

As Mr. Mansfield walked to the front of the house, Ted clumsily undid Thunder's knot. Lila could tell that he was still nervous. She glanced wickedly at the others and sidled up to him.

"So, Ed, you like working with horses?"

"Uh, it's *Ted*. Yeah, um, I guess I like it." He forced a tense laugh. "Excuse me. I should go now." He shifted from foot to foot, as if stuck in place, and looked at the girls. "Would you like to come to the stable?"

"No, I must return to my *Sexy Stableboy* magazine," Lila said with her nose in the air. She and Ellen pranced back into the house, snickering.

"Thanks, Ted," Elizabeth said, "but we've got homework to do. Besides, it's almost dinnertime."

"I'll go with you!" Jessica said.

Elizabeth was shocked at her sister's enthusiasm. Just as she was about to protest, they all caught a glimpse of a maroon van moving through the trees beyond the house.

"Hey, it's Dad!" Jessica blurted out. "Maybe we can all go together."

As the twins scampered around the house, Ted called after them, "OK! I'll be, uh, loading your horse into the Carson van!"

They got to the front of the house before Mr. Wakefield did. Elizabeth smiled guiltily at Jessica. "You know, I think he thinks Thunder belongs to me," she said. "Boy, is he shy!"

"Yeah?" said Jessica with a glint in her eye. "I think he's cute!"

Elizabeth rolled her eyes. It didn't seem very long ago that Jessica was saying how gross all boys were.

A few seconds later, Mr. Wakefield got out of the van. Steven, who had just finished basketball practice, was with him.

"Hi, Dad! Hi, Steven!" Jessica said. "Before we go home, can we follow this horse van to Carson Stable? The stableboy invited us. He's a neat guy, and he's in your class, Steven. And you'll love the stable, Dad! It's incredibly huge."

Mr. Wakefield's dark eyes sparkled. He knew what Jessica was like when she had her heart set on something. "OK, OK! We have a little time. As long as it's all right with the stable people."

Jessica waved to Ted, who was guiding Thunder into the horse van. When he was done, he came up to Mr. Wakefield's window.

After Jessica introduced Ted to Mr. Wakefield, the boy said, "I asked your daughters if you'd all like to come visit the stable."

"Sure, Ted. For a little while. We'll follow you." He stuck out his hand. "This is my son, Steven. Jessica says you two are in the same class."

"Hi, Steven! Yeah, you *do* look familiar. I've seen you play! You were great against that forward from Big Mesa," Ted said easily.

Steven perked right up when he knew Ted recognized him. "Thanks. Do you play sports?"

Ted smiled sadly. "Wish I could. We can talk more when we get to the stable."

Elizabeth wondered what Ted meant by that strange answer. But as she watched him walk back to the horse van, it became clear. Ted bounced up and down unevenly with a slight limp.

Even Steven was impressed when they pulled into the stable. "Pretty big place," he called out the window to Ted.

"Mr. Mansfield is going to show you around," Ted said. "I have to straighten up the tack room, and then I'll be right with you."

They all got out of the van. Mr. Wakefield, Steven, and Elizabeth went over to join Mr. Mansfield on his way to Thunder's stall. But Jessica stayed behind.

"Go ahead, you guys," she said. "I want to see the tack room."

Elizabeth nodded, but she was the only one who really knew what was going on. *She doesn't even know what a tack room is*, she thought, as she watched her sister walking with Ted, Jessica gabbing flirtatiously, Ted red-faced and fumbling over what to say.

The two of them entered the small wooden shed. Jessica looked around at all the bridles, saddles, and crops hanging on the walls and lying on tables. There were also saddle pads, blankets, bottles of liniment, jars of saddle soap, brushes, currycombs, and hoof picks. She had no idea what any of it was used for.

"I've never seen so much, uh, tack," she said.

Ted fidgeted and looked around. He couldn't stop stumbling over his words. "Oh, right. Um, this is one of the biggest selections of cattles—I mean, collection of saddles—in Southern California."

"No kidding. I guess you have to know a lot about horses to work in a place like this."

"Well, it's the only thing I really love. I want to be a horse trainer some day."

"But you told us you were saving up for college. Do you need to go to college to be a horse trainer?"

Ted's face turned red. "I lied. I just didn't

want to lose this job, and I thought that sounded better . . ."

Jessica found his pained confession touching. She looked at him, but he coughed and averted his eyes. "You know," he continued awkwardly, "I really am sorry about scaring your sister. She seems so nice, I'd never want to hurt her."

"That's OK, Ted. She got over it. It was an honest mistake."

"Yeah? Good, 'cause it's hard to see someone so, you know . . . pretty and nice . . . being so angry."

"We're identical twins. Can you tell?"

"Yeah, you two do look a lot alike." Jessica smiled as he searched for the next thing to say. "I don't think I ever saw a girl as pretty as Elizabeth."

Jessica's heart sank. *And what am I, the ugly duckling?* she thought. She was beginning to feel annoyed at her sister. First Elizabeth had stolen away Lila, and now Ted wanted to talk about nothing but her.

Ted noticed that something was bothering her. That made him even more nervous. "Not that you're not . . . you look pretty good . . . I mean, you know what I mean— *Whoa!*"

In his state of confusion, he had backed into a case full of equipment. Down he went, followed by a shower of jars and brushes.

There was a moment of stony silence. Then Jessica began to giggle. Ted's fall seemed to loosen up something, and a small smile crept onto his face too. Before long they were both on the floor, clutching their sides in uncontrollable laughter.

Jessica looked into Ted's blue eyes. His face was twice as handsome now that he was relaxed. *Maybe he was just trying to compliment me*, she thought.

Suddenly Elizabeth appeared in the doorway and looked bewildered at the mess inside. Ted sprang up and said, "We'll be right there, Elizabeth. As soon as I clean up this mess."

Then again, Jessica said to herself, with a jealous glance at her sister, *maybe not*.

Seven

◇

The next few weeks were heaven for Elizabeth. She enjoyed writing her article about Thunder, and she managed to finish it during her lunch periods. That left most of her afternoons free to give the horse his daily workout. And each day, when the final bell rang, she would jump out of her seat and rush to the stable.

Usually the first person she saw there was Mr. Mansfield.

"Whew, that's a speed record today—fifteen minutes from the end of school! You sure you don't keep a horse with you in class?"

Elizabeth smiled and headed for Thunder's stall. A large new sign on the stable wall caught her attention:

CARSON STABLE ANNUAL OWNERS' EVENT
BEGINNERS, INTERMEDIATE, ADVANCED
COMBINATION EQUITATION/JUMPER
PRIZE MONEY!

Maybe I should tell Lila about this. Thunder would be an easy winner, Elizabeth thought. She read the date listed at the bottom of the sign and figured out that it was just under a month away. She looked up at Thunder and tried to imagine Lila practicing and getting excited about competing. No way. She wouldn't be the least bit interested. It would be just a waste of time to mention the competition.

She tacked Thunder up and walked him out to the ring. But she couldn't go in because some stablehands were working there.

"Sorry, Elizabeth!" shouted one of the workers. "We're setting up the beginners' jumps now. We've got some owners who're gonna try them later on. Are you gonna enter the competition?"

"Uh, no, I don't think so. I'm really busy next month." She couldn't bear to tell the truth about it.

She took Thunder into the pasture and rode him for a while. In the distance she saw Ted taking a large bay around at a breakneck gallop. His form was flawless, and the control top-notch as he brought the horse to a smooth stop.

"Ted!" Elizabeth cried.

"Hey, did you get a load of Chester? He's the strongest one we've got here. Watch!"

As Ted galloped away, Elizabeth marveled at his riding ability. Never had she seen anyone that young with so much skill on a horse. *That's the way I want to be someday,* she thought.

Elizabeth took Thunder through an energetic workout. When it was over, she waved to Ted and rode back to the stable.

But as she passed the ring, she had a sudden urge. The workers had finished, and there were no riders practicing in the ring yet.

"Should I?" she asked herself. As if in answer, Thunder vigorously nodded his head. She took that as a sign. "OK, big guy, if you say so."

And with a slight pull on the right rein, she steered Thunder into the ring to try the beginners' jumps.

In less than a month, Elizabeth and Thunder became stars at Carson Stable. They cantered with such agility that some of the stable workers took breaks to watch them. They switched gaits with ease and grace. They did effortless figure eights, changing leads from one side to the other with just the briefest trot in between. Elizabeth's seat had become picture perfect, and Thunder seemed happy to obey her every cue.

When Elizabeth finished her workout, many of the stable workers shouted words of encouragement.

"Nice seat!"

"Well ridden!"

"Hey, any time you want to sell that beauty . . ."

They all think I own Thunder, she thought. And it was no wonder. She had been the only person riding him for the past three weeks. Still, she felt a little funny about not telling anyone the truth.

She walked Thunder back, and Ted strolled up beside her. "You're looking better and better every day," he said.

"Thanks, Ted, but I've got a long way to go before I get to your level."

"Maybe, but I started when I was really young. This is the only activity I've ever done outside of school. For you, it's just a matter of time."

Elizabeth had been dying to ask Ted a question, and now seemed like a good time. "Ted, why did you get so interested in horses? Did it have something to do with your leg?"

She noticed his shoulders straighten up self-consciously. But he looked right at her and answered her question. "Two years ago, my parents and I were driving home on the freeway when we were hit by a drunk driver. My father had some head injuries, and my leg was hurt. It never did get back to normal."

"And your mother?"

Ted lowered his head. "We . . . we lost her." He looked at Elizabeth with tears welling up in his eyes. "She was a great horsewoman."

Something dawned on Elizabeth. "Anita Rogers," she said. She remembered reading about her.

Ted nodded. "That's her."

"Well, she was a real role model, Ted. No wonder you're so good."

He smiled. "And I'll never give up. Anyway, with this leg, there's no other sport that I can do!"

"Do you still have your mother's horses?"

"No, we had to sell them to pay the hospital bills. But I've been saving up all my life for a horse, and I'm pretty close to having enough for a down payment."

"Can your dad help you?"

"Well, he doesn't make much, but he told me he'd help with the upkeep if I ever bought one."

Elizabeth grew thoughtful. They walked along together in silence for a while. Then Ted straightened up.

"Elizabeth, I've been watching you practicing your riding techniques. Have you signed up for the beginners' event in the owners' competition?"

"Uh, no, I haven't." Elizabeth felt rotten about not telling Ted that she really wasn't Thunder's owner. But she just knew he'd hate her if he found out she'd been holding this secret so long. "I . . . I have too much to do that weekend."

Ted shrugged his shoulders. "That's too bad.
You really have a good chance to win. I'd hate to
see the blue ribbon and seventy-five dollars go to
someone else!" He looked at his watch. "Well, I'd
better get to work again. See you!"

As Ted went off, Elizabeth's head was swim-
ming with all kinds of mixed feelings. On the one
hand, she was thrilled that someone as talented as
Ted had complimented her on her riding.

On the other hand, she didn't like deceiving
everyone. But it felt wonderful to get all this attention at the stable. And it was too late to admit the
truth now. They'd all think she'd lied to them.

Added to all of this was the situation with
Lila. Elizabeth had to pretend to be friends with
Lila just so she could ride Thunder!

One of these days she would have to come
out with the truth. But when Elizabeth looked at
the course in the ring, she had a hard time fighting
temptation.

I could enter that competition, she thought, *and
no one would ever have to know.*

Eight

BRRRRING! Jessica thought it was awfully early in the morning to be getting a phone call. She ran into the kitchen and picked up the receiver. "Hello!"

"Hi, Jessica. It's Lila."

"Oh, hi there! What's up?"

"I was calling for Elizabeth. Is she around?"

What? She doesn't even want to speak to me first! "Elizabeth? Uh, sure, Lila, I'll get her."

Jessica walked upstairs to Elizabeth's bedroom. The door was closed tight. Softly, almost at a whisper, she said, "Liz. Phone."

A couple of minutes later she heard Elizabeth walk downstairs, humming. Then the humming stopped.

"Jess!" she heard from the kitchen. "Why is the phone off the hook?"

Jessica nonchalantly opened her door. "It's for you. It's Lila. Didn't you hear me call you?" Then she closed it again.

"No! How long has she— Hello! Hello, Lila?"

Lila wasn't used to waiting for people, and she sounded like it. "It's about time, Liz. *I* have to get ready for school too, you know."

"I'm sorry, Lila. It's my fault. I didn't hear Jessica calling me!"

"So I gathered. Listen, I had a couple of questions about that science project . . ."

Behind her closed door, Jessica couldn't hear what Elizabeth was saying. *The Unicorns were right. Those two are getting to be good friends now. They can't even wait till school starts before they start talking.* She quickly got ready and walked out the front door while her sister was still on the phone.

"Jessica? Jessica? I'll be ready in five minutes!" Elizabeth called after her. But Jessica had already gone.

"Listen, Lila," she said into the phone, "it must be getting late. Jessica already left. I'll see you at school. Bye!" With that, she hung up and ran upstairs to get dressed.

At school, Jessica didn't meet Elizabeth at any of their usual places. Elizabeth could sense the reason why. After lunch she came face-to-face with her in the hallway.

"Hi, Jessica. Can we talk?"

"Sure, but make it quick. Betsy wants to show me pictures of her new boyfriend."

"I know what you think about the phone call this morning. Lila wasn't ignoring you. She was just in a panic about the science project."

"Well, I hope you straightened her out. See you later!"

"Wait!" But it was no use. Jessica was already lost in the crowd of students.

Jessica continued to stew the rest of the day, until she ran into Lila before last period.

"Hi, Lila, long time no see!" she said with forced sweetness.

"Oh, Jessica! Did you get a load of the outfit on Cammi Adams today? Polyester city!"

"No, I haven't noticed. By the way, are we still going to the Dairi Burger after school today?"

"The Dairi Bur— Oh, you're right! That was supposed to be today! I forgot all about it and made other plans."

Jessica was starting to boil. "Oh? And what plans are those? Are you signing up to join *The Sweet Valley Sixers*?"

"Jessica Wakefield! What *are* you talking about?"

"Well, Lila, I just thought you might be spending some more time with my sister, that's all. At least I *think* she's my sister. I hardly ever see her anymore."

Jessica tried to sound as if she were joking,

but Lila sensed something wasn't right. "Oh, Jess, you don't have to get so upset. I still like you just as much as I always did."

"No, no. That's not it!" Jessica said, feeling silly for having brought up the subject. "Forget I said anything."

"Well, no matter," Lila said with a smile. "I'll make it up to you. I'm going to have a slumber party this Saturday—just a few girls. And you're the first one I'm inviting."

"Great! I would *love* to come to your party." Jessica felt much better now.

That evening Elizabeth came home from the stable just in time to have dinner. Mrs. Wakefield was in the kitchen as she came through the front door.

"Hi, Mom, I'm home!"

"You're getting later and later every night, Elizabeth."

"I'm sorry, Mom. Where's Jessica?"

Mrs. Wakefield sighed. "Upstairs. Where else would she be when I need her in the kitchen?"

"I'll help you finish, Mom," Elizabeth said. "Just let me change out of my riding gear."

"Is Ted here?"

"Yeah, he's in the backyard. I think Steven wants to show off his jump shot."

"Well, the first thing you can do for me is

rescue Steven from the jaws of basketball after you change."

Elizabeth laughed and went into her bedroom, just as Jessica emerged from hers, wearing a sweat suit and slippers.

"Hello, Lizzie. How was Thunder today?" Jessica asked pleasantly.

"Uh, great! I've been starting to do some jumping. Only two feet, but—"

"That's nice," Jessica said as she made her way down the stairs and then turned toward the kitchen.

Well, at least she's talking to me, Elizabeth thought.

Mrs. Wakefield raised an eyebrow when Jessica came into the kitchen. "Are you coming to help or to taste? If it's to taste, you're too early. And if it's to help, you're just in time."

It *was* to taste, but Jessica knew she was stuck now. She had run out of excuses for getting around helping with dinner.

She went over by the window to get an apron. She gazed outside. Suddenly, she gasped in horror. There, watching Steven shoot baskets in the yard, was *Ted*.

Instantly, helping with dinner became the last thing on Jessica's mind. All she could think about was that her hair was a mess and her clothes were all wrong. She darted out into the hallway.

"Where are you going?" Mrs. Wakefield said. "I thought you were going to help!" She knew it was too good to be true.

"You didn't tell me *he* was coming to dinner!" Jessica cried as she raced up the steps.

"Ted? Yes, that's why I need the help!"

By this time, Elizabeth had changed, and she figured out what was going on. "I'll be right there, Mom," she called.

Jessica frantically tore off her sweats and put on the first decent outfit she could find—a lavender jumpsuit. Then she ran up to her mirror and fussed with her hair. She was furious that no one had told her Ted was coming. *I would have shown up to dinner looking like Godzilla*, she thought.

Jessica was the last one to sit down to dinner. She entered the dining room looking as fresh as the lemon blossoms outside—and smelling like them, too.

"Ted!" she exclaimed. "I didn't know you were coming. What a surprise!"

"Some surprise," Steven said. "I mean, you *always* come to dinner smelling like a fruit basket, don't you?"

Jessica glared at him and sat down.

"I saw you making a couple of good fifteen-footers out there, Ted," said Mr. Wakefield.

"Uh-huh. Uh, thanks! Steven's trying to convince me I can play basketball."

"He's got potential!" said Steven.

Elizabeth felt proud of Ted. She knew what a good athlete he was. "And you should see him on a horse!" she exclaimed. "Kentucky Derby, watch out!"

"Well, you're not so bad yourself," Ted said.

Ha! I bet she tried to steal him away too, thought Jessica.

But now that they had all gotten on the subject of horses, Ted was starting to open up. In no time, everyone started to feel comfortable and happy. Even Jessica.

"You know, Ted," she said, "I have to admit . . . that day you showed me the tack room, I had no idea *what* you were talking about."

Ted smiled. "That wasn't hard to figure out."

"But I had fun," she added.

"Well, you might like horseback riding. Why don't you come out to Carson again? I'll give you a lesson."

Jessica didn't know whether she wanted to go that far. But Ted's offer made her light up inside.

Soon everyone had finished eating. Ted stood up. "I'll help clean up," he said.

Just as Elizabeth was about to volunteer to help, Jessica cut her off. "No, no. Sit, Lizzie. I'll help."

Ted took in a load of plates and started rinsing them. Jessica circled the table, picking up glasses.

"Jessica, what a treat!" Mrs. Wakefield said, exchanging a knowing glance with her husband. "Gee, we ought to invite Ted over more often."

Jessica made a face and put the dishes down in the kitchen. When she went back to the dining room to get the silverware, Elizabeth was getting up from the table.

"Well," said Elizabeth. "I've got a lot of stuff to do if I'm going to go to the party Saturday night."

Jessica stopped in her tracks. "What party?"

"Lila's slumber party. Lila told me you were going, too. Aren't you?"

That did it. Jessica dropped the forks and knives onto the table and bolted out of the room and up the stairs.

Nine

◇

Jessica was steaming. She couldn't believe that Lila had invited Elizabeth to her slumber party too! When had the two of them become such good friends?

Before long there was a knock on the door, and Mrs. Wakefield came in.

"OK, would you like to tell me what's the matter? You've got five very worried people down there."

Jessica's face was buried in her pillows. "I don't care. I'm never leaving this room as long as *she's* in this house!"

"All right. All right. Why don't we start at the beginning? You haven't been yourself lately."

"*Me?*" Jessica shot up from her bed. "What about *Elizabeth*? *She's* the one who hasn't been herself, or haven't you noticed?"

"Just a minute, young lady. Remember, you're not too old to be grounded. What do you have against your sister these days?"

"Oh, Mom, I don't mean to yell at you. But it's just that . . . well, ever since Elizabeth went to see Lila's horse, things haven't been the same."

"I figured this had something to do with Lila."

"I'm so sick and tired of hearing 'Thunder this' and 'Thunder that.' All Elizabeth wants to do is be around that stupid horse. But she didn't have to steal away my best friend to do it!" Tears welled in her eyes.

"Jessica . . ."

"And what makes me so mad is that she's only *pretending* to like Lila," Jessica continued. "I know how she really feels about her! And not only that—" She stopped, full of pain and confusion. She just couldn't admit how she felt about Ted.

"What, honey? What else?"

"Oh, never mind!" Jessica could hold it back no longer. She burst into tears.

Mrs. Wakefield sat next to her and gently put her right arm around her shoulder. "I understand, Jess. But maybe your sister isn't completely to blame. Don't you think you ought to have a talk with Lila?"

"I guess so. But she makes me so mad. She made it sound like she was inviting me to a special party with just a few of her best friends, and now it turns out that she invited Elizabeth too!"

"Well, it sounds like she wants to be friendly with *both* of you. I can understand that." Mrs. Wakefield kissed Jessica on the forehead. "Look, sweetie, you're just going to have to learn to share your friendship. After all, Elizabeth and Lila *do* have a common interest, and they have every right to be friendly."

"OK, Mom, you're right. I'll try."

Mrs. Wakefield gave her a hug. "That's my girl. Now get yourself together and come say goodbye to Ted."

Jessica nodded as her mother left. But inside she was thinking, *Some "common interest!" Each one takes advantage of the other.* She wiped the tears off her face and straightened up.

Oh, well, she thought, *I may as well say goodbye to Ted. After the way I just acted, I'll probably never see him again.*

That Saturday, Elizabeth and Jessica went to Lila's together.

Mr. Wakefield dropped them off at the Fowler house, and they walked up to the front door, clutching identical duffel bags.

"Jessica, is this going to be all Unicorns?" Elizabeth asked. She was beginning to have cold feet.

"Probably. I mean, most of Lila's friends *are* Unicorns. Don't worry, though. I'm sure you and Lila will find lots to talk about. You have common interests."

As soon as they walked inside, Elizabeth's worst fears came true. There they were, practically the entire Unicorn Club: Betsy Gordon, Tamara Chase, Kimberly Haver, even Janet Howell, Lila's cousin and the eighth-grade president of the club.

"Hurry!" said Kimberly, as she pulled on Jessica's hand. "You're just in time for the new video by Frontal Lobe!"

They hurried through the foyer and ran into the TV room. Elizabeth lagged behind them. The video didn't look interesting to her—just a bunch of skinny men with makeup, clutching guitars and sticking their tongues out at the camera. *What am I doing here?* Elizabeth thought as the girls squealed with delight at the TV.

"Aaaawwgghhh! They are the *cutest*!" screamed Kimberly.

"I like Zeke Paranoia the best! Don't you?" Betsy said as she turned around and came face-to-face with Elizabeth.

"Oh, hi, Elizabeth. I didn't realize you were here."

Now all the girls turned around. There was a weak chorus of hi's and hello's, and they all turned back to the TV.

Lila jumped to her feet. "Liz! Mrs. Pervis finally made chocolate chip cookies! You want some?"

"Yes! I mean, thank you, I would." As Lila went into the kitchen, Elizabeth sat down with the rest of the girls. She looked at the TV. Another video. This time a group was singing with tortured expressions on a windy cliff.

The whole thing just seemed silly to her. But she desperately wanted to fit in with the girls. "What group is this?" she asked.

Tamara Chase looked at her as if she were from Mars. "Hyper Ventilation, of course. Haven't you seen this video before?"

"Oh, yes, I must have. Mm, they're good!"

"Aah, they're not so great."

The music videos seemed to go on forever. Not even the chocolate chip cookies made it easier for Elizabeth to take. Finally, Lila announced it was time for bed.

With great excitement, they turned off the TV and ran into Lila's bedroom. *Now maybe we can talk about something interesting for a change,* Elizabeth thought.

But no such luck. Just as Elizabeth had always thought, quiet time was gossip time for the Unicorns.

"So, Betsy," said Janet, "how was your date with Lloyd Benson?"

Everyone giggled and made a face as Betsy answered, "Eeww, stop it, Janet. Just 'cause you saw him bump into me at the mall . . . He has a hard time walking straight without his computer!"

"I know! He's weird," said Tamara. "We ought to fix him up with Amy Sutton."

"No!" shouted Janet. "He's so blind, he might think Amy's hair is a mop and dunk her in a bucket!"

As the girls fell on the floor in hysterical laughter, Elizabeth was burning inside. How dare they make fun of Amy?

Betsy caught her breath long enough to say, "She'd probably clobber him first with her field-hockey stick! Poor Amy. You think *any* guy would ever like her?"

Elizabeth couldn't sit still and take this anymore. She felt as though she was about to explode. "Well, somebody *does*! You all weren't at Julie Porter's party last week, when Ken Matthews *kissed* her!"

There was a moment of shocked silence. And immediately Elizabeth knew she'd said something she shouldn't have. She had meant to defend Amy, but instead she'd revealed her friend's deepest secret.

"*Kissed* her?" Janet said. "I hadn't heard about *that*! That's juicy, Elizabeth."

"Listen," Elizabeth began, "I shouldn't have

said that. All of you please promise me you'll never tell anyone, OK?"

They all nodded their heads reassuringly. *Fat chance*, thought Elizabeth.

The night was unbearable for Elizabeth. She couldn't fall asleep. Every time she closed her eyes, all she could see was Amy, looking angry and hurt. It wasn't until the sun had started to rise that she finally dozed off.

The next morning, everyone awoke and went into the kitchen for breakfast—everyone except Elizabeth.

"Wait a minute. Where's Liz?" Lila said.

"I woke up once in the middle of the night, and she was still awake. I think we should leave her alone," Tamara said.

They ate a big breakfast and said goodbye to one another. As Mary left, she noticed Jessica right behind her. "You're leaving too?" she asked.

"Sure, why shouldn't I?" Jessica asked casually.

"Well, your sister's still here, isn't she?"

"She knows the way home. Besides, who knows when she'll wake up?" The way she felt about Elizabeth, Jessica would just as soon let her fend for herself.

When Elizabeth woke up and saw it was noon, she nearly hit the ceiling. "Lila! Where are you? Where is everybody?"

Lila came into the room. "Good afternoon, Rip Van Winkle! They all left a couple of hours ago."

"Oh, I'm so sorry! I never sleep this late. I had trouble getting to sleep."

"So I heard."

Elizabeth started to get dressed. "Thanks for a great party, Lila, but I've really got to go. My parents must be wondering where I am."

"Don't worry, Jessica told them. Besides, you can't leave now."

"Why not?"

"Well, I've been reading over your article about Thunder and me, and there are a few things I wanted to talk to you about."

"I thought you said it was perfect. Anyway, I wanted to finish retyping it so I could turn it in tomorrow."

"Great! That gives us time."

"Well, not really, because—"

Lila's eyes pierced right into Elizabeth. "I think I've been very generous with my horse. You *do* want to keep riding him, don't you?"

Elizabeth swallowed hard and sat down. She had the feeling she was sinking deeper and deeper into this mess.

Ten

◇

"Elizabeth! Elizabeth!"

From behind her in the school lobby, Elizabeth heard Amy's voice. She didn't know how she could face her after what had happened over the weekend. And she felt even worse when she turned around and saw Amy. Leaning on the wall next to her was Ken.

"Hi, Elizabeth," said Amy. "Is the paper all ready for today?"

"Uh, yeah, Amy, it is. I finished it up this weekend, and I'm going to give the typed masters to Mr. Bowman before lunch."

"Where do you find time to do all this?" Ken asked. "I don't even have time to do my homework."

Elizabeth smiled. "I guess it's because I want

to be a writer someday. It's good to start practicing early."

"I still think it's pretty incredible." He looked at his watch. "Well, I'd better get to my locker before class starts. See you, Elizabeth."

As soon as Ken was gone, Amy gave Elizabeth a sly smile. "This is so weird, Liz. What should I do?"

"What do you mean?"

"You know . . . Ken and me! I mean, we've been good friends for a while, but now!" She noticed Elizabeth was looking at the floor. "Come on! I told you what happened at Julie's party. He must really like me, right? But he never says anything about it! Should I bring it up or wait?"

Elizabeth wanted to confess to Amy that she had told the Unicorns her secret. But she felt so confused, all she did was say weakly, "Maybe you should wait. I don't know."

"Hey, you seem a little down today. What's the matter? Newspaper deadline blues? Don't worry, everything's going to be fine."

"Yeah, you're right. Thanks, Amy."

"Thank you. You know, I'm so glad I have someone I can share my secrets with. If anyone else knew what happened at that party . . . Ooh, I think I'd die!"

It was exactly what Elizabeth didn't want to hear. Now she could only hope that for once the Unicorns could keep a secret.

*   *   *

Elizabeth dragged herself through the rest of the day. She didn't even feel much relief when she handed in the masters for *The Sweet Valley Sixers*. It wasn't until she got to the stable after school that she felt like her old self.

"Hey-y-y, how are you doing?" Ted called out to her as she walked to Thunder's stall. "He's going to be excited today! He hasn't seen you in a couple of days!"

"I know. I missed him!"

Elizabeth brought Thunder out and started to walk around. Ted joined her. "Guess who's coming to dinner tonight?" he said.

"Dinner? Where?"

"At your house. Give up? Steven invited me over again."

"That's great, Ted. We can leave here together."

As soon as Elizabeth got on Thunder again, it was as if the weekend had never happened. He was full of spirit, and gentle as always. And Elizabeth was feeling more and more comfortable when she took him over the cavaletti and the small post-and-rail in the ring.

At five-thirty the Wakefield's maroon van pulled up to the stable. Mr. Wakefield tooted the horn twice lightly, and Elizabeth and Ted hopped in.

Steven was waiting in front of the house, basketball in hand. When the van stopped, he waved Ted into the backyard, and the two of them immediately started to play basketball.

Elizabeth and her father headed toward the house. The smell of lasagna filled the air, as Mr. Wakefield jogged into the kitchen. "We're home, Alice! Just in time for me to make my famous Caesar salad."

As he got to work on the salad, Jessica reluctantly set the table. Elizabeth changed her clothes, and Mrs. Wakefield called out the kitchen window, "Come on, boys! Dinner's almost ready." Out of the corner of her eye, she caught a glimpse of Jessica sneaking upstairs to her room. "Jessica, go lightly on the perfume this time," she cautioned gently.

"Who won?" Jessica asked Ted with a smile when everyone had sat down to dinner.

Ted laughed. "Steven, of course."

"Yeah, but you're getting a lot better."

"You were really hard to stop along the baseline! You must be something on the horses."

"He is!" said Elizabeth.

"I guess it runs in my family," Ted said modestly.

Jessica gave Ted a coy look. "I don't know. I think Ted looked better than Steven out there."

"How do you know? You didn't even see us!" said Steven, sneering.

"I peeked," said Jessica. "Ted, would you like some salad?"

"Sure!"

Steven shot Jessica a look of disgust. "Look, magnolia blossom, don't you think you ought to go put on some more perfume? I'm beginning to be able to smell my dinner."

These days Jessica already had a short fuse. She didn't need her brother to set her temper off. "At least I don't smell like a locker room!" she exclaimed.

"Jessica, Steven!" Mr. Wakefield said evenly, his brown eyes glaring at Jessica and Steven. "We have a guest here."

An uncomfortable silence settled over the table. After a few moments, Ted started on a new subject.

"You should see your daughter on Thunder, Mr. and Mrs. Wakefield. I keep trying to convince her to sign up for the owners' competition, but she won't listen to me. She's a sure bet to win first prize in the beginners' event."

"*Owners'* competition?" Mrs. Wakefield said.

"I know why she's not entering the owners' competition," Jessica declared. "Because she's *not* the owner! Thunder's Lila's horse. Elizabeth's just taking care of it! You mean you never told Ted, Lizzie?"

Elizabeth sank into her chair. She'd never been more humiliated in her life.

Eleven

◇

The next day Elizabeth felt devastated. The last thing she wanted to do was face Ted at the stable after school. She tried all day to think of a good excuse to stay away. But it was tough. Her next set of riding classes didn't start until the following week, and the homework that night was light. Besides, she'd always come back to the same thought. What about Thunder? It would be heartless to ignore his daily grooming and workout.

When the final bell rang, Elizabeth dragged herself out of school and took a long, slow walk to the stable. She rehearsed about seventeen ways of apologizing to Ted.

Her stomach sank as the Carson sign came into view. She shuffled up to the front gate and looked both ways. Ted was nowhere to be seen. She walked through quietly, and scurried to the office. Mr. Mansfield was sitting behind the desk. "Hi, Mr. Mansfield," she said in a small voice, and ducked into the locker area.

"Evening, Elizabeth! Sounds like you've got yourself a little sore throat there."

Please, not so loud! she thought as she closed the door and changed. She didn't want anyone to know she was there, at least not until she was ready to go home.

She rushed out to the stable and peeked in the door. No one was there. With her head bowed, she entered Thunder's stall.

The big horse turned to look at her with one deep brown eye. He seemed to sense something was wrong.

Elizabeth just wanted to throw her arms around him and cry. But she bit her lower lip, clasped her hands in front of her, and stopped right beside him.

"I—I'm sorry," she said tenderly. "I'm just a greedy person, I guess. And a big liar to boot. Oh, I know I should have told everyone the truth. But you have to understand . . . I felt so proud when people thought you were mine! Besides, we both know that Lila couldn't care less about you. And I've given you care and love, haven't I?"

"Yes, you have."

Elizabeth jumped with fright. She whipped around to see someone familiar crouching by the stall door and giggling.

"Ted!" she cried out, half in relief and half in fear. "You sneak, you scared me!" But as soon as she saw the impish look on his face, she laughed.

"Things must be tough, if you're talking to a horse!" he said with a friendly chuckle.

"Well, Ted . . ." She looked down at her hands. For a moment, the words just wouldn't come out. It was as if they were stuck in her mouth. She was almost sick with embarrassment. She wanted to run away and never come back.

"What? Is something really wrong?"

She raised her head to face him, her eyes brimming with tears. His face looked so sincere, so intent. And suddenly the words rushed forth as though they were going through a broken dam.

"Oh, Ted, how can you be so sweet to me after last night? I bet you've never met anyone this sneaky. All along I never told you the truth about Thunder. I kept it from you on purpose. I *liked* pretending that I was his owner! It was just one big, fat lie!" She sighed. "Now you see why I can't enter the contest."

There. It was over. She'd said it.

Ted just stared, with a puzzled look. "So?" he said.

"What do you mean, *so*?"

"I mean, so what if you don't own Thunder?" said Ted. "It doesn't bother me. Besides, the owner can select a substitute rider, and that's even *more* reason you should enter the contest."

"How do you figure that?"

"Well, first of all, I've always stayed away whenever Lila came to visit you at the stable. That girl gives me the creeps. All this time I couldn't understand why you'd invite her here. But I *have* noticed that she never seems to come around on Fridays."

"Of course not. She's always going out on Fridays." Then she understood what Ted meant. "And the contest is on a *Friday!*"

"You're right about that!"

"And you can always give her the prize money if the whole thing bothers you."

His argument made a lot of sense. And it sure was a big relief that he wasn't angry at her.

"Then . . . you don't mind that I was lying to you?"

"No way. I know how you felt. Besides, I lied to you when I said I was saving up for college, remember?"

Elizabeth felt as though a huge weight had been lifted from her shoulders. "Yeah, I remember."

"So, what do you say? Are you going to enter? The event is this Friday!"

"Will you be my trainer?"

"You bet!"

Elizabeth grinned so wide it almost hurt. "OK, you're on, but under one condition!"

"What's that?"

"This stays between you and me and the people at the stable. I don't want anyone else to know."

"It's a deal! I'll meet you in the ring in half an hour." He let out a little whoop and went back to his work.

Elizabeth looked at Thunder and said, "What do you say we get ready?"

Thunder nodded his head and snorted. Maybe it was just a coincidence, but Elizabeth didn't think so. She knew that Thunder understood.

After Thunder was warmed up, she took him to the ring. Ted was every bit as good a coach as Elizabeth thought he would be. He put her through a demanding workout, constantly giving her tips and shouting encouragement. But it made her a little scared. There were so many things to learn!

When it was time to go, Elizabeth was exhausted and a little worried. She paused for a minute atop Thunder. "How am I doing?" she asked Ted.

He slowly walked up to the horse and rested his hand on the skirt of the saddle. "Well, let me tell you something . . ."

Ted looked right into her eyes and said, "Elizabeth Wakefield, if you don't win this competition, it'll be the biggest shock of my life."

*   *   *

The next day at school, Elizabeth was nearly exploding with happiness. There were times when she would let out a loud giggle in the middle of the hallway. People were beginning to stare at her.

Everyone must think I'm crazy, she thought. *I don't know how I'm going to keep this a secret.* She was dying to tell someone. She had always confided in Jessica, but that was out of the question these days. Besides, she had sworn Ted to secrecy, and she couldn't very well go blabbing everything herself.

By the end of the day, Elizabeth had managed to calm down a bit. She had convinced herself that she was completely back to normal.

Until she ran into Amy between classes.

"Hey, Elizabeth, what's going on?" Amy said. "What are you smiling like that for? Did I button my blouse wrong?"

Elizabeth laughed. She wanted so much to tell Amy. "No, no. Your blouse is fine. How's everything with Ken?"

"Oh, pretty good, I guess. He asked me to walk to school with him, because he doesn't live too far from me."

"Mm-hm, that's good," Elizabeth said. But it was clear her mind was on other things.

"Elizabeth, you are acting weird! Is there something you want to tell me?"

That was all she needed. She grabbed Amy by the hand and led her off into an empty corner of the hallway. "Amy, you have to promise me you won't breathe a *word* of this to anyone. Including my sister."

"I promise! What is it?"

"I'm entering Thunder in the owners' competition at Carson Stable this Friday. I'm really not supposed to because he belongs to Lila, but she wouldn't care anyway. And after it's over, if I win, I'll give her the prize."

"That's fantastic! Can I come cheer you on?"

"Sure!"

"I can't wait!" She started to rush off to class, then stopped and turned around. "There's one thing you're doing wrong, though."

"What's that?"

"I think you should *keep* the prize!"

Twelve

Friday seemed to be the toughest day of Elizabeth's life. It was torture to have to wait through a whole day of school. Her favorite subjects all seemed unimportant. She could think of one thing only.

And the worst part was that she couldn't tell a soul about it. Each class seemed to go by slower than the last. At times she felt like standing up and screaming. She wished *everybody* could know about the competition. But she kept it all secret—even from Jessica, who didn't seem to suspect a thing.

Thank goodness for Amy. Every time Elizabeth saw her, the two of them would exchange a wink or a smile. Elizabeth had almost forgotten what had happened at Lila's party. It looked as though the Unicorns could keep a promise after all.

As the end of the day got closer and closer,

Elizabeth began to count the hours to the competition. She was glad her teachers weren't calling on her in class, because she wouldn't have been able to answer. Her body may have been at Sweet Valley Middle School, but her mind was already across town at the Carson Stable.

After the final bell had sounded, Elizabeth had the strangest feeling as she walked to the lobby. It was as if everybody and everything were underwater. All the sounds were muffled, and the people just seemed to be floating around her.

But when she saw Amy she snapped back to normal. "Come on, Elizabeth, get it together! You look like you're in the Twilight Zone. Don't tell me you're nervous!"

Elizabeth's eyes brightened as she said, "Nervous? No, just excited. More excited than I've ever been."

Together they rushed out to the front of the school. Amy took Elizabeth into a corner near some hedges. She clasped Elizabeth's shoulders with her hands and looked right at her.

"Remember, whatever happens today, you know I'll be rooting for you. You're going to be great, so stay loose and show 'em who's best!"

The two girls gave each other a hug, and Elizabeth headed in the direction of the stable to prepare for the event. Then Amy went back into the school and walked toward her locker. She didn't have much time before she had to leave, too.

As she crossed the lobby, she noticed something that made her go cold. A crowd of Unicorns had been looking at her through the glass doors, and they were whispering to each other. Among them were Lila, Kimberly, Tamara, and Betsy. Amy tried to ignore them, but as soon as she passed by, they started to snicker.

Amy snapped around to face them. She didn't have much patience for this sort of thing. "What's so funny?" she said.

"Oh, nothing, Amy. Can't anyone laugh a little?" Lila said. All the girls now had very serious expressions.

Amy started to leave. At that moment, Tamara turned to the others and puckered her lips as if she were kissing someone. Betsy couldn't keep a straight face and burst into laughter. That made the rest of them break up, and in an instant they were all cackling and trying to cover their mouths.

Amy threw her books down on the floor and went right up to Lila. "All right. What's going on? Why don't you guys grow up?"

"Oh, it's *so* hard to be as grown-up as Hot-Lips Sutton," Tamara muttered to Betsy.

Amy glared at her. "What was that, Tamara? I couldn't hear you."

"None of your business. What makes you think I was talking about you?"

"You girls all think you're so special. Well, you're not. You're *boring* to everyone but yourselves.

What's so great about sitting around all day, showing off clothes and talking about boys, anyway?"

As Amy started to storm off, Kimberly said, "I guess you're way past the stage of just *talking* about them."

Amy stopped dead in her tracks. Lila started to titter, and Tamara made slurpy kissing noises.

"What are you idiots talking about?" Amy said. It was impossible that they could know anything about . . .

Lila stepped forward with her hands on her hips. "Idiots, huh? Well, I guess we boring girls just aren't as cool as Amy Sutton. Not one of *us* has ever kissed Ken Matthews, the midget."

Amy's jaw dropped open. She didn't know whether to be furious or embarrassed. She tried to speak, but no words came out.

"Oh, don't just stand there looking so innocent," Lila continued. "Elizabeth told us all about it!"

"She did not!" screamed Amy. Not in a million years would her best friend rat on her!

"Oh, no? Then maybe we heard her wrong. Even though she *did* tell *all* of us, right in my bedroom at my slumber party." She gave Amy a snide grin. "It happened at Julie Porter's party, right? Too bad none of us were invited."

At that point, Amy was starting to see red. "Oh, yeah? You think you're so smart, don't you? Well, you're too stupid to know that Elizabeth is riding *your* horse in a competition right now! And she's gonna win it, too, no thanks to you!"

Uh-oh. Before Amy could keep the words from coming out, it was too late. Lila's eyes blazed with anger.

"Competition? Nobody's going to enter *my* horse in a competition!"

All the other students in the lobby cleared away as Amy, Lila, and the Unicorns ran toward the front doors.

At the stable, Elizabeth was giving Thunder's coat a final going-over with a finishing brush. The rays of the afternoon sun streamed in through the door, making red highlights in his coat. Elizabeth stood back and stared. Sometimes when she looked at Thunder, it was like seeing him for the first time. That same chill would run through her, that same excited feeling of discovery.

"No matter how we do today, I will be so proud of you," she said, and she began to tack him up.

Once the saddle and bridle were in place and the girth secure, Thunder was ready to go. Elizabeth gazed up at him with her proudest smile. "OK, my friend," she said, "nothing can stop us now."

Suddenly a voice broke their privacy. "I wouldn't be too sure about that, Elizabeth."

She turned around with a start. It was Amy. And she looked furious.

Thirteen

◇

"Amy, you scared me! How come you're here so early?"

Amy paced up and down the stable. She was out of breath, as if she had just run a great distance. "You're lucky I'm here at all, Elizabeth."

"What? Is something wrong? Did you *run* all the way here?"

Amy spun around to face her. Her face was twisted with anger and hurt. "Elizabeth Wakefield, how could you?" she cried, the words pouring out. "I thought you were my best friend! I thought we could keep each other's secrets. I never *dreamed* you would tell anyone—not even Jessica. And now I find out all the biggest creeps in the whole school have been laughing behind my back! And it was *you* who betrayed me!"

Elizabeth let go of Thunder's reins and dropped her head. She knew immediately what had happened. It was as if her worst nightmare had come true.

"Please tell me I'm wrong, Elizabeth! Tell me someone else told them!" Amy ran over to Elizabeth, her eyes full of hope. "It was an accident!" Elizabeth cried.

"So it *is* true," Amy said softly. She let her hand fall and slowly walked away. With a deep sigh she said, "Well, if you need to explain anything to me, you'd better do it fast, because any minute now—"

It was too late. Into the stable of horses marched the angry crowd of Unicorns. In front of them was Lila Fowler. "Just *what* do you think you're doing with my horse?" she demanded.

The events of the last few weeks played in Elizabeth's head like a movie on fast-forward. All for the love of Thunder, she had betrayed her best friend, set her own twin sister against her, deceived everyone at the stable, and even managed to make an enemy of the girl who owned the horse. Everything she'd been afraid of had come tumbling down around her. And the competition she'd dreamed of entering was about to begin. What should she do? Apologize? Run away? Get angry? Cry?

"*Say* something, Elizabeth," Amy pleaded.

Elizabeth looked into Amy's eyes. They were troubled, but strong and clear. And all at once it dawned on her.

There was only one thing to do.

She turned her head sharply to face Lila. "I'll say something," she said calmly, "and I'll say it right to your face, Lila Fowler. I'm tired of worrying myself sick about staying on your good side. Of trying as hard as I can to like you and be your friend. This horse means more to me than you'll ever know, but nowhere near as much as my family and my best friend. And definitely not enough to keep playing your games."

Lila's eyes were nearly popping out of her head. She'd never been so humiliated.

"This is your horse, Lila," Elizabeth continued, "and it's a shame you don't know how good he is. He deserves a better owner than you, and I guess I was trying to be that for him. Well, it took a long time, but I've learned the hard way that I can't."

A shocked hush set over the stable as Elizabeth brought Thunder over to Lila and put the reins in her hand.

"I'm dropping out of the competition. If anyone should enter, it's you, Lila, because Thunder is a winner."

All eyes were on Lila, except Amy's. She was looking with admiration at Elizabeth. She felt choked up with emotion. Elizabeth had made a mistake, but she was strong enough to admit it. And that was good enough for Amy.

Lila just stood there for a while. She seemed to be debating with herself about something. Everyone waited for her response.

"Elizabeth," she said softly, "uh . . . do you really think my horse can win this competition?"

"Yes, I do," Elizabeth answered. "And so does everyone else in the stable."

Now Lila looked very interested. "Really? And what would it say on the award?"

"Well, it would have the name of the event, the name of the horse, and the name of the owner."

At that, Lila gave Elizabeth her most engaging smile. "Well, you know, Elizabeth, now I understand what you've been going through. Why didn't you tell me before?"

Elizabeth and Amy glanced at each other. They both knew what was coming next.

"OK," Lila went on, "no more game-playing. I'm *really* sorry I made you feel so terrible. Let me make it up to you. Ride Thunder in the competition. I insist. You deserve it."

Elizabeth threw her head back and laughed. "No more game-playing, Lila? Everything I said went right over your head, didn't it? You just want that ribbon!"

Amy beamed with pride. She wanted to applaud, but she thought that would be rude.

Lila fingered the reins slowly. "So you won't do it, huh? Even though you wanted to so badly?"

Without a word, Elizabeth turned her back on Lila and walked out the stable door, Amy following close behind.

"You know I'll never let you ride Thunder again!" Lila called after her. But Elizabeth kept walking.

"Elizabeth, I want you to know I'm proud of you," Amy said when they got outside. "And I forgive you. You'll always be my best friend."

Elizabeth threw her arms around Amy and started to cry. "Thanks. And I feel the same way."

"Hey, it's OK, Elizabeth. Don't cry. This is a happy ending!"

Elizabeth gave a half-smile. "Yeah . . . almost."

"What do you mean?"

"Well, it's just such a damn shame that Thunder won't be in that show. I know he'll be disappointed, and I wanted so much for everyone in the stable to see him."

Amy thought for a moment. "Hmmm. Is there anyone else who could ride him?"

As if in answer, a voice piped up from behind them. "Hey, Elizabeth, aren't you going to be late?"

It was Ted. Elizabeth and Amy looked at each other with gleaming eyes.

"Ted," Elizabeth said with a sweet smile, "we have an offer you can't refuse . . ."

Fourteen

◇

Ted was all ears as the two girls explained everything.

"So let me get this straight," he said. "You want *me* to take your place in the event?"

Elizabeth and Amy nodded eagerly.

"Well, you have to understand, that would really be unfair!"

Of course. Ted was far too advanced to ride in a beginners' event. Elizabeth hadn't thought that one through all the way. "You're right," she said. Both she and Amy groaned in disappointment.

Ted put his hand on his chin. "Unless . . ."

The girls chimed together, "Unless what?"

"Unless I enter him in the advanced event!"

Elizabeth looked horrified. "With all that jumping?" she said. "I know you're good, Ted, but Thunder's never done that!"

She saw a familiar impish smile on Ted's face. "Don't be too sure," he said.

"Ted! You can't mean—"

"Well, Elizabeth, you're not the only sneaky one around here! I've been taking him out on days when you're not here, and sometimes after you leave."

"No wonder you weren't mad at me for not telling the truth!" she said, laughing. Then she gave him a hard glance. "You're *sure* Thunder can handle those jumps?"

"Like a pro!"

"And you want to enter?"

He blushed a little. "Well, do you think maybe you could get your sister to come?"

Elizabeth smiled broadly. "I'll call her, right after we talk to Lila."

The three of them went back into the stable. Lila was still holding Thunder's reins, but now she was waving her arms around and yelling something to her friends. When she saw Elizabeth and Amy come in, she looked outraged. "Now you listen, Elizabeth—"

"Lila, we have a great idea!" Elizabeth interrupted. "You may win that blue ribbon after all!"

Lila's expression changed. "You mean you'll do it?"

"No way. But if you're interested in getting the biggest prize in the whole event, you'll let Ted enter."

Lila remembered the episode with Ted in her backyard. So did Ted.

"I may not be a 'sexy stableboy,' but I'm sure you won't mind when I win the advanced competition."

"Advanced?" said Lila. "*You* can do that stuff?"

Ted shrugged his shoulders. "Hard to believe, isn't it?" Then he held out his hand for Thunder's reins.

Elizabeth had never seen him so confident. Lila meekly handed him the reins, and they all went out to the ring to talk to the officials.

The stable was bustling with excitement. It was already impossible to get a seat in the center of the bleachers. Car after car came through the front gate, and people parked quickly so they could rush out and be with friends and family. The smell of freshly cut grass wafted past Elizabeth's nostrils as she took in the scene.

She let Ted and the others go ahead while she dashed over to the pay telephone in the office. She called home and the phone rang once . . . twice . . . four times . . . ten times. No one was there.

Where are they all? Elizabeth thought as she hung up. Ted would be so disappointed.

Just as she was about to leave the office, she decided to give it another try. Maybe she had dialed the wrong number. She went back and dialed again.

Again the phone rang and rang. Elizabeth was just about to hang it up when she heard a tiny voice coming out of the receiver. "Hello . . . hello?" It was Jessica!

"Jessica! You're home! I'm so glad!"

Jessica sounded out of breath. "Yeah, we just got in, and I heard the phone ringing from outside. Lizzie, the strangest thing happened today. I went to a Unicorn meeting, and practically nobody showed up!"

"I know! They're all here!"

"What? Where?"

"At Carson Stable! And you better come, too, if you want to see Ted ride Thunder!"

"Ted? Wait a minute, why are the Unicor—"

"It's a long story. I'll tell you later. Just get here! 'Bye!"

Elizabeth raced out to the ring. By now the bleachers were almost packed. She took a seat on the end just as the beginners' event started.

One by one, the owners took their horses onto the track, mounted them, and went through the familiar walk, trot, and canter routine. Then, just as Elizabeth had practiced all these weeks, they all tried jumping the cavaletti and post-and-rail. Most of the owners were around Elizabeth's age, and some of them could handle everything and make the jumps. But none of them could do it as well as Elizabeth and Thunder, and Elizabeth knew it. She felt her heart sink when the winner was announced, but she knew she'd done the right thing.

Halfway through the intermediate competition, Jessica still hadn't arrived. Elizabeth dashed into the office and called home. Again, Jessica answered. This time she didn't sound too happy.

"Jessica, why aren't you here?"

"I can't come!"

"Why not?"

"Mom's still at her office, working late, and Dad's in some stupid meeting with a client in his study."

"Can't you come over on your bike?"

"Dad wants me to stay home and help with dinner. He doesn't understand!"

Elizabeth knew how disappointed Jessica was, but she tried to sound cheerful. "That's OK, Jess. I'll be sure to tell Ted you're rooting for him."

"Yeah . . . OK. 'Bye."

As soon as Elizabeth left the office, she started to feel nervous. She could see the intermediates were almost over. The owners in the advanced division were lining up. Soon it would be Ted and Thunder's chance. They were scheduled third.

Elizabeth sat in her seat and watched Ted prepare. He adjusted the stirrups and chatted with some of the other people in his division. He appeared to be the youngest one by far. As he paced around, Elizabeth noticed the stiff walk he always used when he was trying to cover up his limp. *He's nervous,* she thought.

The intermediate winner was announced. The crowd started to chatter as the jumps in the ring were raised and others were added.

The first horse entered the ring. Elizabeth didn't know the owner, but she recognized the horse. It was Chester, the beautiful bay she had seen Ted ride before. He held his strong head high as the owner took him around the ring. Then, at the owner's signal, he charged toward the jumps.

Elizabeth swallowed hard. Chester was sensational! He cleared every jump with room to spare. The audience let out a huge cheer as the owner smiled smugly. Obviously this horse had become a crowd favorite over the years.

The second horse didn't fare nearly as well. In fact, he refused the brush fence three times and was eliminated from the competition.

At this point, Elizabeth noticed that Ted was looking over toward the front gate. He shot a worried glance at her. But all she could do was shake her head. Ted tried to hide it, but she knew he was crushed that Jessica wasn't there.

He mounted Thunder and headed for the ring. As they trotted once around the track, Elizabeth noticed something was wrong. Ted looked uncomfortable, as if the crowd scared him. That old sureness wasn't there. Thunder was good, but not quite at Chester's level. He cleared the first five jumps, but had a knock-down on the chicken-coop jump. Elizabeth buried her head in her hands. She knew Ted was *much* better than this.

There were six horses left for the second round. The jumps were raised from two-and-a-half feet to three. Again, Chester cleared them all with ease—and again Thunder had one knock-down.

Ted's forehead was lined with frustration. This wasn't at all what he had expected.

The higher jumps proved too much for every other horse. It was now down to Chester and Thunder. The jumps were raised again another six inches. Elizabeth began to worry. *What if Thunder hit one and it didn't fall properly? He and Ted could both be hurt!*

Chester charged again. He cleared the post-and-rail easily, and sailed over the brick wall, the brush fence, and the chicken coop. Then he stormed onward to the in-and-out. But just as he reached it, he refused! A shocked hush went through the crowd, and the owner tried again. For the second time, Chester refused, and Elizabeth's heart started to pound. One more refusal and he'd be eliminated.

The owner was yelling at the horse. He walked Chester back to try again. Fierce determination was in the eyes of both owner and horse. The owner kicked his legs, brought down his riding crop, and they galloped toward the jump with much greater strength than before. Surely they would make it this time.

Elizabeth felt drops of sweat trickle down her forehead. Suddenly her jaw dropped open. At the very last moment, Chester reared up on his hind legs, letting out a huge whinny and almost throwing the rider!

Now it was up to Ted. If he could do it, he'd win the prize. If not, according to the stable rules, they'd have to do it all over again.

He took a deep breath. Fear was written all over his face.

Just then, a car sped through the front gate. Elizabeth's eyes darted over, and she let out a squeal of joy. It was the Wakefields' van! The door was flung open, and out came Jessica, Mr. Wakefield, Steven, and a man Elizabeth had never seen before.

Elizabeth glanced back over to Ted. He had a grin that looked as if it would split his cheeks.

As Jessica sat down next to her, Elizabeth whispered, "I thought you couldn't come!"

"You won't believe this, but all of a sudden Dad and Mr. Lewis rushed out of the study and told me they were coming here! Mr. Lewis had lost track of the time and wanted to see his daughter in the beginners' event!"

"Well, he's too late, but you're not!"

Ted concentrated on the first jump. With a strong kick, he set Thunder in motion. They cleared the post-and-rail with inches to spare. Thunder tucked his hooves beautifully and lifted his hocks at the last minute. Elizabeth gasped.

One by one, Thunder took the jumps as if he wanted them even higher. But the last one still remained. And if Chester couldn't do it . . .

Thunder took off toward the in-and-out. Something about that double jump seemed to scare him, and he refused. Ted tried it again. And the twins nearly crushed each other's hands as he refused again. "If he does it again, what happens?" Jessica asked in a choked voice.

"He'll do it," Elizabeth said, but she didn't quite believe herself.

Ted was breathing heavily. His face showed incredible strength and confidence. He kicked Thunder and snapped the riding crop. Thunder charged toward the jump. The crowd was stone-silent. Elizabeth and Jessica held their breaths.

And, like a beautiful brown bird, Thunder glided over the first rail, took one powerful stride, and pushed off majestically over the second.

The audience roared, and the twins hugged each other deliriously. Thunder had won the blue ribbon!

*   *   *

The twins were bursting with excitement as they walked back to the stable with Ted and Thunder. Even Steven was impressed. "When I heard you were in this competition, I figured I'd come," he said. He gave Ted a crooked smile. "I guess I can see what you like about this stuff."

Ted laughed and said, "You ought to try it sometime. Especially when I start beating you in one-on-one." Steven gave him a playful punch, and Jessica got between them.

"Leave him alone, Steven. Have some respect for the winner!"

They all started talking at once, until the stable door opened and Lila came in.

"Congratulations, Ted," Lila said softly. "You're really good on Thunder."

"Well, Thunder's the best one I've ridden. I guess you'll want to give him a rubdown now."

Lila crinkled her brow. "A what?"

"A rubdown, Lila," Elizabeth said. "He has to have one now, and remember, he's your horse."

"Oh, gross. Won't you do it, please, Elizabeth?"

Elizabeth folded her arms and shook her head. A tense silence filled the air.

Ted looked from one girl to the other. Then he straightened himself up and looked seriously at Lila, as if he were about to say something he'd practiced.

"This may sound ridiculous, Lila, but I may

be able to solve your . . . uh . . . problem," he said.

Everyone looked at him.

"I've been saving a lot of money from my job; it comes out to just over seven hundred dollars." He loosened his collar and swallowed. "And I think that's not a bad down payment for Thunder. I'll give you a little something every month until I'm completely paid up."

Lila looked at him in disbelief. "You want to *buy* Thunder?"

"More than anything else," he said.

She thought about it for a moment. Elizabeth sensed that she was thinking of the nice things she could buy with seven hundred dollars. "It's a deal!" she said. "I've had enough of horses for a while!"

"Oh, Lila, you're terrific!" Jessica exclaimed.

But Elizabeth was shocked. "Don't you want to ask your father first?" she said.

"Oh, he'll agree," Lila said. "I've been thinking of selling Thunder for a long time."

Ted was so thrilled, he jumped in the air.

"Congratulations, Ted," Elizabeth said. She was smiling, but Ted sensed a certain sadness in her face.

"Elizabeth . . . what's wrong?" he said.

"Nothing, Ted, nothing. I'm very happy for you," Elizabeth answered, as she cast a glance at Thunder.

But Ted realized what was bothering her.

"Hey, don't worry, Elizabeth. You can ride him whenever you want."

Elizabeth's face lit up. That was just exactly what she wanted to hear.

Jessica couldn't keep her eyes off Ted. He looked so handsome when he was this happy. She stood alongside him and gave him a warm smile. "And maybe I'll start taking riding lessons, too."

Ted smiled back at her as Steven groaned. Elizabeth was glad to see the two of them finally connecting. She reached for her book bag to get ready to leave. As she picked it up, a slip of paper fell out.

It was Jessica's riddle, from Mr. Nydick's class ages ago. Elizabeth read it and called out, "Hey, Jessica, what room *did* the black stallion check into when he went to a hotel?"

Jessica blushed. "Oh . . . the bridle suite."

This time *everybody* groaned. Jessica shrugged her shoulders. She couldn't be too upset. After all, life was finally going to be normal again.

Fifteen

◇

"Hi, Elizabeth! Remember me?"

Elizabeth and Caroline Pearce were busy getting ready for *The Sweet Valley Sixers* meeting the following Monday afternoon. Elizabeth looked up to see a vaguely familiar dark-haired girl.

"Sophia. Sophia Rizzo," the girl continued. "You gave me change for the pay phone a few weeks ago."

"I remember! You wanted to join the newspaper, right?"

"Yes."

"Great! Well, come on in and sit down. This is Caroline, one of our columnists."

Sophia greeted her cheerfully, but Caroline just nodded coldly in return.

Elizabeth noticed Caroline's reaction, but decided to ignore it. "What kind of articles do you like to write?" she asked.

Sophia quickly pulled up a chair and sat right on the edge. "You name it. Interviews, news, sports. I'd even like to help put the paper together—you know, typing, handing it out to classrooms. Anything!"

Elizabeth gave the girl a big smile. "Well, how'd you like to start with this issue?"

"This issue? Oh, that would be fantastic!" Sophia said as she pulled out a notebook and pencil. "What should I work on?"

Just then a deep voice startled the three girls. "Hey, Sophia! What's takin' you so long?"

They looked up to see a rough-looking older boy standing in the doorway. His hair was long and stringy, and his dirty flannel shirt hung over his pants. A trace of a mustache was beginning to grow above his lips.

All of a sudden Sophia looked embarrassed and sad. "OK, Tony," she said. "I'll just be another minute or so. Wait for me by the pay phones."

"Yeah? Well, it better be a minute. 'Cause in a minute, I'm leavin'. And I don't care *what* Mom says about it!" With that, he walked off, his worn-out work boots clomping heavily on the lobby floor.

"That's my brother," Sophia said quietly. "He goes to Sweet Valley High. Sometimes my mother makes him walk me home after school."

"That's all right, Sophia," Elizabeth said. "Why don't you come by here tomorrow at this time? We'll figure out a good assignment for you by then."

"Thanks. I guess I'll see you after school tomorrow."

As soon as Sophia left, Caroline tugged at Elizabeth's blouse. "*I can't believe you did that,*" she hissed.

"Did what, Caroline?"

"Let *her* join the newspaper. Don't you know about her?"

"No, Caroline. *You're* the gossip columnist, not me!"

"Ugh. She's trouble!"

"What are you talking about? She seems really nice to me. And I've never seen anybody so excited about working on the *Sixers*—"

"Yeah? Well, it's fine with me if you want that gorilla of a brother hanging around here all the time."

"He is kind of creepy. But still—"

"Elizabeth, the whole family is screwed up! She has no father. No one can figure out where he disappeared to. The three of them all live in this tiny house in the worst part of town. And Tony's not only ugly, but *dangerous!* I heard he broke into someone's house to steal a VCR. And I know for a fact he spent last year in reform school. I have a bad feeling about that girl. If you want my advice,

I think we should just tell her we have enough writers."

Elizabeth sank back in her chair. Sophia seemed like such a nice girl. She couldn't very well kick her off the newspaper now.

But something deep inside her understood Caroline's feelings. Elizabeth could sense that trouble was brewing ahead.

Has Elizabeth made a big mistake, or can she trust Sophia? Find out in Sweet Valley Twins #9, **AGAINST THE RULES.**

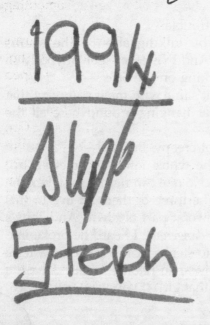